Praise for Ally Kennen's novels:

BEAST

WINNER of the Manchester Book Award
SHORTLISTED for the CILIP Carnegie Medal, the Booktrust
Teenage Prize, the Branford Boase Award, the Berkshire Book
Award, the Leicester Book Award and the Bolton Book Award

"Rings with talent and compelling detail . . . a tense, funny
and touching tale. I really love this book"
Amanda Craig, *The Times*

"*Beast* has a tension that never lets up. Ally Kennen
is already a remarkably assured writer"
Nicholas Tucker, *Independent*

"An extraordinary imaginative achievement . . . this is
a compassionate story from an exciting new voice"
Bookseller

"Sharply and wittily observed . . . An exceptional first novel"
Books for Keeps

BERSERK

WINNER of the North East Teenage Book Award
and the Leicester Book Award
SHORTLISTED for the Manchester Book Award,
the West Oxfordshire Book Award and the
Coventry Inspiration Book Award

"Written with a verve and confidence that never lets up.
Very funny . . . this excellent novel well deserves
the large audience it should get"
Independent

ALLY KENNEN comes from a proud lineage of bare-knuckle boxers, country vicars and French aristocracy. Prior to becoming a writer, she has worked as an archaeologist, a giant teddy bear and a singer and songwriter.

Her first novel, BEAST, published in 2006, was shortlisted for the Booktrust Teenage Prize and the Carnegie Medal, and won the 2007 Manchester Book Award. Her second novel, BERSERK, won the North-East Teenage Book Award and the Leicester Book of the Year Award 2008.

Ally lives in Somerset with her husband, daughter and two sons, three chickens, a curmudgeonly cat and two bloodthirsty kittens.

No woman has ever beaten Ally in an arm wrestle.

Also by Ally Kennen

BEAST
BERSERK
BEDLAM

SPARKS

QUARRY

ALLY KENNEN

MARION LLOYD BOOKS

First published in the UK in 2011 by Marion Lloyd Books
An imprint of Scholastic Children's Books
Euston House, 24 Eversholt Street
London, NW1 1DB, UK
A division of Scholastic Ltd.
Registered office: Westfield Road, Southam, Warwickshire, CV47 0RA
SCHOLASTIC and associated logos are trademarks and/or registered
trademarks of Scholastic Inc.

ISBN 978 1407 11107 0

A CIP catalogue record for this book is
available from the British Library

Printed and bound in Great Britain by
CPI Bookmarque Ltd, Croydon CR0 4TD
Papers used by Scholastic Children's Books are made from wood
grown in sustainable forests.

1 3 5 7 9 10 8 6 4 2

This is a work of fiction. Names, characters, places,
incidents and dialogues are products of the author's imagination
or are used fictitiously. Any resemblance to actual people,
living or dead, events or locales is entirely coincidental.

www.scholastic.co.uk/zone

Remembering the beautiful Meena Reetooraz
05/06/75 – 24/12/09

CONTENTS

1	Happy Ted	1
2	Traffic	6
3	The Dare	13
4	Insects	21
5	Silva	32
6	New Mission	39
7	Dad	47
8	Geebo	56
9	Plane	67
10	Butterflies	81
11	Venus	90
12	Night	101
13	The List	105
14	Frances	119
15	Sheeley	126
16	Café	134
17	Judge	142
18	Friday	153
19	The Villa	164
20	The Ring	170
21	Big Man	176
22	Water Snake	187
23	April Fool	196

24	Boy Missing	202
25	Shot Tower	211
26	Mr Mouse	217
27	Scrappy	224

Happy Ted

I thought he was dead this time.

Sheeley meets me at the gates, out of breath and failing to keep her panic under wraps. "Is Grandad with you, Scrappy?"

"No."

So now I'm tearing around, my heart racing and sweating fear. I live in a breaker's yard. *Happy Ted's Salvage. Happy Ted* is my grandad. He's not so happy these days. Dad runs the show now. The place is chock-a-block with the wrecks and carcasses of cars that have been dented and smashed and written off. There are plenty of places for my mad old grandad to hide.

I check Bella, the crane. Sometimes Grandad forgets Dad has banned him from driving the heavy machinery. Today, thank goodness, Bella sits empty and still, her massive grab resting on the crumpled roof of a camper van. Now I'm scurrying through the dump, checking the piles of cars. Sheeley scoots round the back of the garage to look in the old aeroplane. The cockpit is one of Grandad's favourite places even

1

though the pilots' seats have been replaced by a couple of stools, and the roof has begun to leak. Years and years ago Grandad was an aeronautical engineer; then he got made redundant and he started up this place.

But where is he now? I eye Dad's broad back through the window of the office. He's on the phone. Dad's quite temperamental, and since Mum left (four weeks and two days ago) he's been tricky to say the least. Sheeley gets on with him better than me, but then, she gets on better with everyone than me. I don't want to go in. Dad will be annoyed by me butting in when he's on the phone, but we need help and I'm tipping into panic.

I bang on the door. "Dad, Ted's missing."

I step inside and Dad waves at me to be quiet. He paces up and down, the phone to his ear, and the floor bends and squeaks under his heavy boots. He's wearing his usual outfit, a green and black checked lumberjack shirt over black jeans. His long dark hair, streaked with grey, is tied back with an elastic band. I heard somewhere that you get stuck wearing the same sort of clothes and have the same hairstyle dating from the time when you were happiest in your life. I hope it's not true; otherwise it would mean Dad hasn't got any happier since he was sixteen. Mum said he was handsome when he was young. His old guitar hangs dusty and quiet on a hook on the wall. He was in a band when he was my age. Mum says they were really good, but he doesn't play any more. Dad slams his hand on his table, wanting me to leave. Anyway, old

Ted isn't in here. I go outside, purposefully letting the door slam.

"I'm going up the quarry," shouts Sheeley, climbing through a gap in the hedge to the steep field behind our yard. That's when my sinking feeling gets worse. There's deep, deep water up there.

The office door swings open and Dad flicks his fag into the weedy flowerpot by the door.

"Found him yet?"

I shake my head.

"I've had ENOUGH of this," snaps Dad, like it's my fault his old man is going round the bend. He climbs into his truck, hauling his big body into the seat, and slams the door. He fires her up and reverses, skidding the tyres and spitting mud. He, barely missing Sheeley's yellow mini, belts out through the gates and down the potholed track. In the distance I hear the roar of the motorway. It's two fields down, double fenced. The noise never leaves my ears.

"Grandad?"

That's Sheeley, screaming her lungs out up at the quarry. All this commotion has set Petal off. She's barking fit to bust her gut and jumping and straining at her chain. Grandad wanders off from time to time. The whole family goes into red alert until he is found. He's usually hiding in his cottage, or hunting rabbits with an imaginary gun in amongst the wrecks. But not today.

I'm about to go and double-check his cottage when I see a red blur down in the motorway fields.

A croaking noise comes out of my throat.

Grandad is a tall old man. He's got skinny long legs which bow out when he walks. But now he's running. He's running fast, downhill. He's heading straight for the motorway fence. All I can think is how he's wearing his ENVIRONMENTAL HERO T-shirt. We've all got one. The company which ships the crushed cars to China gave Dad a whole boxful.

I pelt through the yard to the far hedge and notice one of the wide mesh gates is standing ajar. These back gates are two metres high and usually padlocked shut. I pass through. Now I'm running fast over the grass, scattering sheep and lambs. I've lost sight of Grandad as I climb the fence at the bottom of the field. I pass through a well-trodden gap in the hedge and then I see him, wobbling on the wooden posts of the fence. Beyond him is a deep cut through which the motorway traffic roars. It's a steep slope. You have to tread carefully. If you lose your footing you could roll down and right out into the traffic.

"TED," I scream and he waves at me as his head bobs down into the cut. I'm running faster than I've ever done in my life. My legs feel like rubber, like they might give way beneath me. The valley is spread out before me: big long hills, brown fields, shorn hedgerows, and the motorway gleaming like a wire. Above the deepening roar of the traffic I hear a sonic boom break the sky as a jet races, miles above. I stumble, recover, and run on; each breath is like a little burn. I cross the bottom field in seconds. I reach the double fence. The first barrier is made of taut barbed wire, tensioned tight to keep Farmer Roger's sheep in. I climb clumsily, snagging the fleshy part of my palm on a barb, blood soaking into the cuffs of my school shirt. The second fence is post and rail, chicken wire nailed to the bottom half. This was put up by the Highways Agency to stop rabbits and other vermin venturing on to the road.

It hasn't stopped Grandad. I'm running along the top of the cut, one hand on the fence to steady myself. Grandad, somehow, has got himself on the hard shoulder, where he follows the painted line. He walks quickly, his arms hanging loose and bouncing off his sides. Some drivers have spotted him – a tall old man dressed only in a red T-shirt and grey jogging trousers – and take precautions. These cars are slowing; some headlights are flashing. Other motorists fly on, oblivious. Now someone is hooting as a white van forces its way through the traffic, speeding through all the worry at ninety miles an hour. As I reach the bottom, Grandad sees me and moves off fast, like I am an enemy.

Please, please, stay on the hard shoulder, I beg.

Please.

Traffic

"TED," I call in a voice I hope is not going to frighten him. But Grandad gives me the sort of look you might give a stranger and bumbles on. He's shuffling now. He's tired. Old men like him are not designed to run down hills and climb livestock fences.

"Grandad?" I'm walking very fast with nervous, shaky legs. I don't want to run because I don't want to alarm him. I'm terrified he'll suddenly dart into the traffic, which is still charging past. He's about thirty metres ahead. I'm praying he doesn't suddenly decide to cross the road.

"Oh help," I mutter. Then I get a flash of inspiration.

"Hey, Grandad, do you want to come and fly the plane with me?" Grandad looks round, his face all mottled and flushed.

"Who's that?"

Despite everything, I grimace. I made this man's breakfast this morning. I washed that T-shirt. Last night we played snakes and ladders for two excruciating hours.

"It's me, Scrappy. Michael. Grandad, please stop." My

6

hand trembles as I wipe a tear off my cheek. "I thought we were going to have a play with the Fokker this evening. We were going to look at the compressor."

Grandad stops. Grey wisps of hair blow over his face. "Michael?" A clear look comes into his blank old face.

I step up and catch his arm. His skin is cool, wrinkled and soft. "Grandad, what are you doing?" Gently I guide him back from the edge of the road.

"I thought you were a Geebo," he says, looking intently at me. I roll my eyes. Geebos are one of his crazier inventions.

"You're wandering along the side of the motorway," I tell him. "What the hell are you doing? Do you want the police to come and put you away? Do you want to cause an accident?"

I help him up the path, gripping his arm tightly so he can't escape. Below us the traffic speeds up, like witnessing a boy dragging an old man out of a motorway cut is something easy to ignore. Grandad leans heavily on me as we climb back up the steep bank. I have to practically drag him over the fence. I wrap my coat over the barbed-wire fence so he doesn't injure himself. As we struggle back up the fields, it starts to rain. We're both getting soaked, but I don't care. In the deep part of my brain I am replaying a scene in which I didn't reach Grandad in time. I can hear the squeal of brakes. I can hear the screaming. But it didn't happen. And by the time we reach the yard I have managed to wipe my mind free of what could have happened down there.

Sheeley's waiting for us in the yard; she's soaked. Her long hair is plastered against her face.

"I saw you from the hilltop," she says. "I saw you climbing over the fence; what happened?"

I fill her in and she holds her hand over her mouth in horror.

"Grandad, you're a walking death trap," she says. Then she proceeds to tell him off until he swears at her but she doesn't back off.

"I see someone left the gate open." She looks at me meaningfully. "Dad will go mad."

"I'll take him home," I say, wiping the rain out of my eyes.

"This can't happen again," says Sheeley.

We walk down the overgrown track that leads off from our yard, all scudded up with dead leaves and overhanging dried-up nettles. A rabbit darts out in front of us, making Grandad grab for his make-believe gun. We step through a rotted gateway into Grandad's garden. Grandad's cottage needs a lick of paint. Bits of stone are slipping from the walls and the roof is bowed like an old horse's back. The front porch is missing a door and the kitchen window is grimy with dirt. My grandmother died before I was born but she's left some souvenirs. Her ancient rose, with a stem thicker than my arm, curls up a dead apple tree in the back garden. It flowers every summer with deep red blooms twisting high up into the tree. Sometimes, on a still day, the scent from them is even stronger than the motorway fumes. Her flowered jug sits cracked and chipped on the moss-covered wall. It's been there for ever. A plastic washing line, green with mildew, hangs stiffly from a rusted post, and at the bottom of the garden is the derelict chicken coop. The wire is all collapsed and grown into the grass. Dad said she used to sell the eggs. I conjure up Gran, a tall, dark woman, feeding her hens, pegging out washing, pouring out juice from her flowery jug. There's no motorway roar.

She's gone now.

Kicking aside pools of rubbish, I lead Grandad through the door of the cottage. The paint is peeling from the walls of the tiny hallway. Newspapers are stacked up either side, smelling of cat pee and worse. Faded paintings of wartime aeroplanes hang uncertainly on the walls. I enter the kitchen – I never get used to the smell of damp and something rotting. The room has an old electric cooker and a small table. A sink unit sags in the corner. There's a tiny twist of something on the dusty old mat by the back door; I think it is mouse intestine. I'll leave that as a present for Sheeley. Sometimes, when she gets the urge, she bursts in here on a cleaning frenzy.

It's always cold, even in summer. There's a fireplace in the sitting room next door but I don't get round to lighting it very often. Instead, Grandad sits in front of an electric fan heater whilst he watches telly. Sometimes I go in there and find he's got the settings muddled and he's been blowing cold air on to himself for the last couple of days. I find a clean, crumpled T-shirt in a crate of laundry and help Grandad to put it on. Mum used to talk about getting Ted to move into an old people's home but it never happened. Now she's gone and moved out instead.

I swear and shake off the beast which has landed on my right calf. Jasper, Grandad's cat. He's a huge black and white tom who turned up about six years ago. He has big paws and mean staring eyes like a lizard. I hate him. So does Petal. When I take Grandad's tea round, I have to stand guard whilst he eats it, otherwise Jasper would have it off his plate. He's always spraying his dirty man-cat stuff around the place, working his tail like a pump. He sleeps in Grandad's bed, and leaves decapitated mice and birds all over the place. He eats two tins of cat meat a day and if he doesn't get fed, he attacks you.

"I'll feed you in a minute, rat-weasel," I tell him.

Grandad's in his chair in the sitting room and I'm passing him a cup of tea when there is a crash in the doorway.

"Where is he?"

Me and Grandad stare at each other. Grandad slowly raises a cushion and puts it over his face. I tense and wait.

Dad explodes into the room, red-faced and sweating.

His hair has come out of its ponytail and straggles over his shoulders.

"Hi, Dad," I say quietly. I haven't seen him in here for ages. He says he doesn't have time. He goes straight over to Grandad. He grabs his shoulders and shakes him hard.

"You stupid idiot," yells Dad. He puts his face right up against Grandad's. "You DON'T WANDER OFF." Specks of spittle land on Grandad's face.

"The motorway is for CARS," he howls. "You stay in this cottage, right? You stay here. You could have caused a pile-up. You could have killed someone." He carries on, calling Grandad all these horrible, horrible names. Me, I'm hovering at the back of the room trying to be invisible, holding two cups of tea. I'm gripping one of them by the rim and it's burning my hand but I don't want to move.

Finally Dad lets go of his shoulders and glares at me.

"You never leave the gate unlocked," he spits, his eyes wide and staring.

"Sorry," I mumble.

It's no use denying it was me. Once Dad has an idea in his head, he won't let it go. Besides, it was me who left the back gate open. Yesterday I'd hammered the old Ford Escort round the lower field, sliding round and round in circles, pretending I was banger racing. The Escort somehow escaped Bella's claw, years ago. It's not roadworthy but it can still belt along. Dad turns a blind eye when me and Sheeley go for a burn round

11

the field – not that my sister is interested these days. The farmer who owns the field, Bill Rogers, doesn't seem to mind as long as there's no livestock in there.

To my relief, Dad stalks out. I set the tea on the carpet and suck my hand. Then I go and pat Grandad's shoulder.

"Sometimes I don't know what I'm doing," says Grandad in a small voice. He's shaking.

"Me too," I say. "Me too."

Dad's doing something to the front door. I can hear the handle rattling and thumping. Cautiously I go out into the hall to investigate.

"I'VE TIED IT SHUT," roars Dad from outside. "SO YOU'LL BLOODY STAY PUT."

"What about me?" I call out nervously.

"CLIMB OUT THE WINDOW." I listen as Dad's feet splash off down the path.

"Sorry," says Grandad. "I'm trouble, aren't I?"

"You certainly are," I say.

The Dare

I was born on April Fool's Day. Maybe that's why nobody takes me seriously even though I'll be sixteen in two weeks' time. Everyone calls me Scrappy, even my sister, Sheeley. My real name is Michael Singer, but it's almost obsolete. Mum, when I see her, calls me Scrappy just like everyone else. I'm not keen on either name. When I get to eighteen I'm going to change my name by deed poll, though I still haven't decided what to. I could either go normal – David, Will, James – or wacky – Antonio, Magic, Elderon – or Irish – Conor, Liam, Aidan (my great-grandad was Irish so it's allowed). I change my mind all the time. When I was little, Mum called me Mr Mouse, because she said I was always creeping around, up to something, and scuttling away if anyone appeared. I'm happy to get rid of that nickname.

Grandad has always called me Michael – when he remembers who I am.

"It's me, Michael," I say, sticking with my birth certificate for now. "Come out, Grandad, I've got your dinner."

It's late on Wednesday evening, a few hours after the motorway incident, and Grandad is hiding under the bed. He's really making a day of it. He's still freaked out by Dad's little pep talk. Sheeley has gone to see a mate in town and I've cooked tea for Dad and Grandad; an omelette. Ted wouldn't care what I put in front of him but Dad is well fussy. He has to have his dinner delivered first because he gets grumpy if it is cold. I gave him his food and he waved me away without even a thank you. I got a surge of anger then. Dad acts like he's in charge of some multi-million pound corporation instead of this stupid little salvage yard. What's he got to be stressed about? I hate having to tiptoe around him all the time. His greatest fear, apart from a heart attack, is that the taxman will come unannounced and ask to see the accounts. That's why he's got Petal, the dog. She guards the dirty money that Dad stashes under the floor of an old transit van. He thinks none of us know about it. No one, not even a dog whisperer, smelling of fresh bones and old cats, gets past Petal. She takes her duties very seriously. It's one way to save, I suppose.

"That cat," says Grandad, bringing me back to the present. "He wants to eat me."

"No he doesn't," I say, though I wouldn't put anything past Jasper.

Grandad hauls his bony body out from under the bed. He sits up straight and rubs his head. His eyes seem to clear and right away he's more like the old

14

Grandad, not the crazy confused one who has appeared on and off for the last year.

"What was I doing under there?" he asks.

"Hiding from Dad?" I suggest.

"I wish he'd leave me alone. I don't want him round here." Grandad gets up, sits on the bed with a squeak as the mattress sags under him. "You should come more often," he says. "I get lonely. I've got things I need to get out."

I help him up. "I've got school, Grandad. I do my best."

Earlier, I climbed out of the sitting room window and cut the rope which was holding the door shut with a bread knife. We can't lock Grandad in. There must be a law against it. And if I hide the key to the back gate, at least that should stop him wandering on the motorway again.

"I don't want Sheeley looking after me, either," mutters Grandad. "She can be a right bossy so and so." He's wearing his pyjama bottoms, one sock and the shirt I gave him earlier. He smells like a toilet. He doesn't allow anyone but me to give him a bath and I don't get round to it very often. Mum said the council should pay for a nurse. Grandad is Dad's father. Mum says Dad should take more responsibility for him. I'm not sure that's such a good idea. Sheeley used to do loads for Grandad but lately he's taken against her, which she finds upsetting. I find it annoying as it means I have to do everything for him now.

I get Grandad downstairs, give him his omelette and sit him in his old armchair with the telly on, then leave him to it.

"Why can't you stay?" asks Grandad. "You don't care about me. None of you do, least of all your dad. He's forgotten about all I did for him. What if the Geebos come when I'm on my own?"

"I've got homework to do," I say.

"You're a wicked lad," says Grandad. "You're wicked like your father."

"Bye, Ted," I say. Then I belt out of the room before he can say anything else. If I listen to him moaning too much, I start to get angry. I shut the door, go upstairs and drag the dirty sheets off the bed. Outside I take in deep draughts of air. Although motorway-fumed, it is a relief from the dank, sour smell of the cottage. As I'm walking back to the yard, struggling with my foul-smelling load, an idea occurs to me. I try to push it to the back of my mind. It's not a nice idea, but it would be quite funny. It would give Grandad something real to moan about. Stop right there, I tell myself firmly. What sort of person would want to wind up their confused old grandad?

Our flat is built over the top of a triple garage where Dad and Olly dismantle the cars. We have a small sitting room, a narrow kitchen, a tiny bathroom and three bedrooms. My bedroom is little more than a box room; there's only space in it for my bed and my cupboard.

16

My window looks out over the yard, and beyond that, to the motorway. The walls are thin and all day you hear machines whirring and blades slicing and hammers banging below. And when Bella gets going, pounding and smashing the cars, the noise is almost unbearable. The roof is made of a kind of tin which amplifies the rain. It has rained harder and longer this winter than for a thousand years. That's what everyone is saying, anyway.

All the noise drove Mum crazy. She was always threatening to move back into the plane. She'd been saying that for years. But it wouldn't be any quieter there because of the motorway being so near and because of the dog, Petal, being a dog and woofing all hours. When Mum and Dad married they didn't have any money for a house, and didn't want to share the cottage with Grandad, so they lived in the plane. It's a Fokker 27, a Friendship, and it dominates the back yard. It's got a wingspan of twenty-nine metres and a turboprop engine. Dad says it takes up too much space, but I love it. It used to be a coastguard plane in Iceland, but twenty years ago it got decommissioned and sold on to a cargo company. The pilot tried to do an emergency landing on the motorway. The landing gear went wrong so it took off again and did a crash landing in the hillside just beyond our yard. It ended up being dragged down to us. There's still a big gap in the hedge where it was bulldozed out to get the plane through (the double gateway through which Grandad escaped).

17

Grandad was paid plenty of money to store the carcass and it's still here. The passenger cabin is big enough for a stove, a living area and a sleeping area and I was five before we moved into the new flat. Now the plane sits mouldering, surrounded by car parts and brambles growing up round it, and Dad sometimes threatens to smash it up for the metal. But everyone knows the plane is me and Grandad's place.

I get a text message as I'm carrying Grandad's sheets back across the yard. I've got my arms full so I can't check it straight away. I walk into the garage, picking my way over bits of engine and pools of oil. We've got a washing machine tucked away in the kitchen unit at the back of the garage. This is where we clean all the overalls and rags, and Grandad's clothes, so we don't have to bring them into the flat. I shove the sheets into the machine, add a double helping of powder and turn it up hot.

Dad appears just as I'm finished.

"Sorry about earlier," he says, trying to placate me. "He drives me crazy. Thanks for the omelette."

I nod. I don't want to talk to him. He always does this, blows up and then expects a few calm words will nullify everything.

"Maybe the rope isn't such a good idea," says Dad. "I don't expect he'll do that again."

"I've undone it already," I say, looking him in the eye.

Dad clears his throat. "I'm taking some seats to Exeter," he says. Dad's always off delivering parts to customers. There's big demand for salvaged car parts and he likes to escape from the yard. We all do.

When he's gone I check my message. I read it, then read it again. It must a joke, an early April Fool.

I DARE U 2 KILL SOMETHING WITH RED BLOOD. REWRD. £50.

I hold my breath, feel myself frowning. What? Kill something?

The sender is unknown. I think it might be from Silva Moxley, my mate. He's into mischief making. All the same it makes me feel uncomfortable, like someone is watching me. I look out at the dark yard, eyeing the shadows between the broken cars. I look away down the hill to the motorway. I watch the headlights stream up and down. *Kill something with red blood?* Isn't all blood red? This is a very sick dare. Does he mean me to snare a rabbit or something? Obviously I'm not going to do it, but I can't help thinking about what I would do with fifty pounds. Maybe buy something for the plane. Me and Grandad are trying to make the old engine work again. I know a bit about engines and Grandad used to work with aeroplanes, though his memory isn't very reliable. We're not wanting to make the thing fly. We just want to make the engine roar. It might seem pointless, but to me it would feel like raising the dead.

I text back.

WHO R U?

But I get a message back saying the number is unavailable. Whoever sent me that freaky message wants to stay anonymous. It must be Silva. He's probably laughing his head off right now. I'll have to pay him back for this.

There's something irritating me, scratching away on the edge of my thoughts. I'm worried that the dare isn't from Silva at all. There's another candidate. And if he's got it in for me, then I've had it.

I'm scared it's from Judge.

Insects

WOOF WOOF WOOF WOOF. Whirrrrrrrrshhh, whirrrrrrrrrrrrr shhhhhhh, WOOF WOOF WOOF, whirrrrrrrrrr shhhhh. WOOF WOOF. WOOF WOOF, **WOOF**. Whirrrrshhhhhh.

This is what I hear all day long – and all night, Petal being responsible for the woofs and the motorway being responsible for the other. And of course, there's the generator. It whirrs away constantly. Dad says we're off the grid, like it's something to be proud of, but it means there's a constant hum in the background and the lights flicker and we get power surges and cuts. If we don't keep the generator topped up with diesel, we get no power. That's no light, no heat, no TV, no phone, nothing. It's a bloody pain. I'd love to live somewhere quiet. Ears are too close to the brain. Whatever comes in through them has a hotline to your mind, interrupting and messing with your thoughts.

I get out of bed. There is only a thin strip of carpet between the bed and the wall, and I edge down this, stepping over the piles of books, and turn to face the large mirror hanging on the back wall. Sheeley laughed

21

at me when I came home with this. She said she never knew I was so vain. But I need it to reflect some light into my room. I want it to be as bright as possible. All the same, I find myself staring in it every morning.

Right now a pale face stares back at me. I've got scruffy dark hair and my cheekbones stick out. It doesn't take much to imagine the skull beneath the skin. The eyes are dark, watching me warily. The eyebrows are already too big. I'm not bad-looking, but there is too close a resemblance to my dad for my liking.

I have a new little habit. I call it my magic. Sometimes it works and sometimes it doesn't. Some days, being Scrappy just doesn't seem to work. I can't think of the right words to say to people or I just make a fool of myself. But my magic helps me out with all that. I stick my tongue out at my reflection.

Who am I going to be today?

WOOF WOOF. . . WOOF WOOF. . .

It's stopped, yes, it's stopped.

WOOF WOOF.

They should use this for torture sessions. It's driving me mad.

WOOF. . .

"SHUT UP, PETAL." (Sound of window slamming.)

It's obviously driving Sheeley mad too. When I enter the kitchen, she's spitting and fizzing like she's eaten a jar of coffee powder. "Can you believe it," she says. "Mum's only gone and filed for divorce."

22

I can believe it. I saw the letter from the solicitor. It arrived on Friday and Dad left it lying on the kitchen table. He didn't mention it to us, of course.

"Why hasn't she TOLD ME?" fumes Sheeley.

"You should be pleased," I say, though I am gutted about it too. But we both know the marriage has been on the rocks for a long time, though we never believed Mum would work herself up to move out. For the last few years Dad has been sleeping on the sofa or in the office and Mum has hardly seemed to be here at all. She works at a youth hostel on the moors and stays there a lot. In the old days she worked in our yard with Dad and Grandad, but that was ages ago.

Something tells me this isn't the right time to show Sheeley my mystery message.

"I'm going round there this morning," says Sheeley furiously. "She needs to keep us up to date. Want to come? We need to sort out about Grandad. She might have some ideas."

Mum's moved in with the caretaker of the youth hostel. He's called Jez and I've known him for years. I used to think he was all right. Now I don't think I could stand to look at him.

"I've got school," I say.

I'm staying out of this. I've got enough to worry about. I put some toast under the grill for me and Grandad. Some days Grandad is completely normal, and will make his own simple meals; other days he doesn't eat at all unless someone takes him stuff. Dad always has breakfast at the service station. He has a bacon sandwich and three fried eggs every morning. When I was little, it was the biggest treat in the whole world to go with him. On those rare occasions, me and Sheeley would sit with our bag of crisps and watch Dad wipe the grease from his mouth as he talked with the lorry drivers. I haven't had breakfast with Dad for a long time.

"Don't be too hard on Mum," I say brightly. "She's probably feeling crap."

Sheeley looks at me suspiciously. "That's not what you were saying yesterday. Yesterday you called her terrible names."

"I'm a better person today," I say.

It's true. Today I am trying to be good. I'm trying to be all cheerful and considerate like, say, my mate Silva's mum. Becky. She never has a bad word to say about anybody. Today I am Scrappy/Becky. I will be kind and positive. I will absolutely not cuss my mother or play stupid jokes on my grandad. I'm even wearing some Becky-like clothing – I have sun-yellow socks on under my school trousers and a colourful "ethnic" wristband Sheeley gave me when I was twelve.

"I'm off," says Sheeley, pulling on her orange coat. "Don't forget, Grandad needs milk and tea bags." Sheeley's studying fashion at college and wears some mad clothes. She grins at me, her bad mood gone. "I'm going flat hunting this afternoon." Sheeley's planning to move out as soon as humanly possible. She's saving up for the deposit but doesn't make much from her job in a clothes shop so it's taking longer than she'd like.

I don't want her to go.

I smear chocolate spread over Grandad's toast. He loves this stuff. Maybe it will put him in a delightful mood and I'll be able to escape in time for school. But there's always something, like he's fallen out of bed, or peed in his trousers. Or he wants to tell you about life in "the old days" or Jasper has brought in something dead, or, worst of all, he's lost the TV remote. I try not to let it wind me up. It's not his fault he's old, but I do get this knot of anger in my stomach.

"I'll drop off the toast," says Sheeley. "Let's see if Grandad remembers who I am this morning."

Outside in the cold wet morning my retinas seem to fog up like steamed windows and everything is blurred. It's raining, of course. Rain is big news. It has rained here every day for thirty days, nearly non-stop. Recently a cheeky little stream sprung up at the bottom of the yard, next to Petal's transit. It runs under the fence into the lane. Sheeley says she's never seen it before. The ground is so saturated there's nowhere for all the water to go and some kids at school have had their homes flooded. We live on a hill, so we're safe, but the big river in Gaunston is swollen and fast. Me and Silva are hoping the school will flood and we'll get sent home.

*

25

I'm collecting my bike from the garage when I trip and crash to the oily floor. I've stumbled over a pair of legs, dressed in grubby blue overalls and steel-toe-capped boots. As I sit up my knee rings with pain.

"Watch it," booms a voice from under a crumpled Fiesta. I'm about to say something rude in response but then I remember I am being Becky-like today.

"Sorry ." I grab my bike and exit. Olly works for my dad. He's been around for ever. He used to work full time but now he says he only wants to be here for two or three days a week. He doesn't talk much. He must be at least sixty. I half wonder if he is behind my freaky message, then dismiss the thought. I don't think Olly has ever owned a mobile phone, and anyway, it's not his style. I run my bike through the rain-soaked yard. We've got police cones, traffic lights, columns of tyres and a mountain of engine parts. Wrecks are stacked five cars high against the border fence. It's a salvage yard, it's never going to be a tourist destination, but I swear it never used to look like it does now, with the fence curling with age, the paint peeling from the walls and black mud nearly a foot deep in places. There are two pots by the office door. Mum used to plant flowers in them. Now Olly's fag butts float in a rainwater soup, not a flower in sight.

As I'm opening the gate I hear a low, rumbling growl coming from the transit parked up beside it.

"Good morning, Petal, beautiful, silken-coated beast. Would thou liketh a nice steak for thy breakfast, oh beauteous canine?" The back doors of the transit are open and inside I see the gleam of two canine eyes. Petal's an Alsatian and she's a lunatic. We have to keep her chained up because she's so unpredictable. Dad got her from one of his mates a couple of years ago, who said she'd been kicked out of the police force for bad behaviour. It doesn't take much to set her off. She even growls at her own reflection in the van window. Dad named her when he was feeling especially humorous.

"On my return from my place of education, I will collect for thee a nice piece of meat from the butcher's establishment," I tell the hound. "Pray, do not savage anyone today, unless he be from the Inland Revenue." Petal shrinks back into the gloom and with a cheery, Becky-like wave, I pedal off between the high hedges of our dead-end lane, avoiding the potholes and ducking arms of mildewed brambles. Through the leaves I hear the motorway. It's at its loudest between eight and ten in the morning and then from four till six in the afternoon. The plants are stunted because of all the carbon monoxide. We get loads of blackberries in the hedge in the autumn, but Mum would never let us eat them. She said they were poisoned by the car fumes. I hope that doesn't apply to me too, and that I haven't grown up as poisoned as the blackberries.

At the end of our lane there's a crossroads and here I turn right and freewheel downhill, and soon I arrive at the roundabout which bridges the motorway. Gaunston services sits just up on the hill. Our yard can be seen on the opposite slope. I stop on the bridge, dead centre, and look down. On the side some joker has painted the legend

SLOW DOWN OR DIE.

The highway agency tried to scrub it off. They cordoned off two lanes of the road and got a couple of blokes with climbing ropes and helmets. They were bouncing around like they were up a cliff. They were there all day and the traffic came to a standstill for hours and hours but the words are still readable.

In the third lane I see a gleaming Jaguar; then my eye is caught by a rusted old Volvo floundering along in the nearside lane. A dirty yellow hippy bus, pouring out black smoke from the exhaust, struggles to overtake. A tired-looking woman driver in an electric blue Mitsubishi glances at me before she sweeps under the bridge. I wait. I always wonder if I'm going to see a crash. I know, it's sick of me, but in my trade you can't help it. All my life I've seen mangled cars dragged into our yard. It's normal. The motorway lamps switch off, one by one, which means it's officially morning. No crashes today. Not yet.

I'm hot. I wrestle off my blazer and send a pile of textbooks crashing to the floor. Mrs Dawson, my French teacher, glares at me with true hatred. You can tell she's suffering too. Her cheeks are red and she keeps taking gulps of water. She's an enormous woman with massive breasts which rest on her desk. She's so fat you can't tell

28

where her legs end and her bum begins. I find myself wondering how much the woman must eat to maintain her body mass. She's opened all the windows even though it's March. The radiators are blasting out heat. The posters on the walls are curling and my mate Silva is drawing pictures on the table with his sweaty finger. Judge is sitting at the back of the classroom. I swivel round and glance at him. He stares back, humourless. He's good-looking, arrogant and deadly. I steer clear of him. I hope the text message wasn't from him. Why would he bother with me? I'm no threat to his autocracy. He's reigned over this school for so long even the teachers have given up trying to pull him in. Anyway, soon Judge will be toppled from power by outside forces. Soon the school won't exist. After our exams it's going to be flattened. There's only us in year eleven left. The sixth form shut down two years ago and all the younger kids didn't come back after the Christmas holidays. Now they go to a big half-finished academy school on the other side of town, with twice as many pupils. We weren't moved because it's our exam year, but as soon as we leave, KERPOW! The whole place will be demolished.

"Miss, I'm going to *die*," moans Alisha, who has taken her shoes and socks off and is wriggling her toes. "*Je suis MORT. C'est très très chaud.*" The class groans in agreement. Things are always going wrong in our school. Lights don't work, the rain drips in through the roof in the main hall and drains overflow. The science block has been fenced off and no one is allowed in any more. We don't know why.

Dawson, damp patches under her arms, caves in. "Silva, go and see if you can find Mr Dayo and ask if he can do something about the heating." Everyone cheers but Mrs Dawson stamps us down by announcing an immediate test on irregular future tense verbs.

Silva always gets the plum jobs. Everyone likes him; even the teachers; even me. He doesn't get stressed and he always looks like he's pleased to see you. He winks at me as he leaves the class and shakes out his hair. It's long, like a girl, like Dad's. I wonder if that wink was about the text message.

Dawson's warbling away and I'm yawning and struggling to concentrate when I notice something fall out of a crack in the Styrofoam ceiling. I strain to see what it is and, losing my balance, tip myself over to the floor.

"Get UP, Michael," roars Dawson, her fat cheeks going even redder. There is a tittering from my classmates as I scramble into my seat. I find myself thinking evil, evil thoughts about her. No, Scrappy, this is not who I am today. I am being Becky-like.

"I am so sorry, miss," I say. I take a deep breath. "I like your shoes, miss."

There is a long, long silence. Shane Buckerell looks round, puzzled and frowning.

"Thank you," says Dawson wearily. The test continues and my ears burn. I'm not cut out for this

Becky behaviour. I idly gaze at the ceiling and screw up my eyes to see better. A large brown bug is crawling over the ceiling. It isn't a spider, the legs are too short. It's not a moth either, no wings. It's a long brown beetle thing, with nasty feelers wobbling around. I watch as it progresses over the ceiling and stop breathing as it comes to a halt right over Mrs Dawson's head.

"Michael," screeches Mrs Dawson and I swear my bum leaves the chair in surprise. "You haven't written a word. . ." But now another bug has emerged from the hole and is feeling its way over the ceiling. I clamp my hand over my mouth as it drops to the floor, landing with a nasty click.

"What's got into you?" the teacher demands. But the door flies open and Silva bursts in.

"Everyone's got to get out, now," he announces breathlessly and the fire bell screams in our ears.

Silva

Everyone mills around in the playground as Dawson screeches orders and the other teachers dribble out of the building. The rain has eased to a mild drizzle, which contributes to the holiday atmosphere. Mr McNealy, the head, comes strutting out in his fusty brown suit. He's always saying that unless we do our homework and work hard, then we'll end up on the scrap heap. I wonder, then, what he makes of me? I was born on the scrap heap. And anyway, it's not such a bad place to be. People should be careful what they say. I look for Frances Hooper. There she is, with a gaggle of her mates, sheltering under a pink umbrella. I've fancied Frances for ever but we've barely exchanged a word.

Someone shrieks and points and we all look to see a van parking up by the tennis courts. It has *PESTAWAY* printed on the sides.

"Maybe it's rats," says Silva thoughtfully. "Rats can carry plague." Then he gets distracted. "Look at that." He winks meaningfully at Melissa Hotbridge's bum. "What a lovely sight," he sighs. This is typical of Silva. Here we are in the epicentre of a school disaster, and my best mate is eyeing up a female. And what a female. Melissa is at least thirteen stone, and shaping up to be another Mrs Dawson. She's pretty enough if you like pale blonde types, and she's very well developed, but she'd squish Silva if he went near her. But Silva doesn't discriminate; he'll go out with older girls, younger ones, girls that everyone else thinks are rough, as well as the angels. He hasn't got a bad word to say about any of them. I nudge him for the secret of his success but he just shrugs.

"No such thing as an ugly flower, man," he says. "They all smell sweet to me."

We watch as a couple of blokes in white outfits climb out of the van. The deputy head, Miss Krill, goes to talk with them.

"It's a terrorist attack," says Shane Buckerell. "We're victims of biological warfare. Any minute we'll be herded into the gym, stripped naked and hosed down with disinfectant." A couple of girls giggle. I watch Judge and his crew. They're sitting on the wall and laughing. I accidentally catch Judge's eye; he sneers at me and nods like he's asking me a question. I look away. Having Judge look at you is like in *The Lord of the Rings* when the dark eye at the top of Mordor switches its evil glare on you, and you know all is lost. Judge is an asshole. He can't stop himself putting people down in a big way. It doesn't help that the big dick is good-looking, loaded and pretty sharp. Rumour has it that he has a list of names. If you do the smallest thing to annoy him, you get yourself written down. Then, in time, bad things happen to you.

"SILENCE," roars Mr McNealy. "Mr Dayo has discovered an infestation, which is most likely not dangerous to anyone, but in the current climate of hyper-allergy we have been advised to evacuate the school whilst it is fumigated. Therefore, I am sorry to announce that the whole school is to be closed as from eleven hundred hours until further notice."

McNealy said other stuff too, but nobody heard because of all the cheering. The teachers gave up trying to control us then. They just shrugged at each other and went to huddle in groups. Teachers are not made for the outdoors. You take them out of their strongholds, surrounded by their power sources – their white board, their cupboards and their laptops – and they come to pieces like a wet tissue.

Silva pipes up. "What's infested the school, sir?" The playground falls silent again to listen.

The head clears his voice. "It's not important," he says. "What is important is that you all take this unexpected opportunity to catch up with coursework and revision. Your exams are very close now."

"Is it so bad, sir," Silva asks, "that you can't tell us?" He's always this cocky. I don't know how he gets away with it.

McNealy ignores him. "Hurry up," he says. "The last thirty pupils off the premises will be given extra homework." The playground clears fast after that.

I hang around with Silva for a bit up town, just chatting about stuff. I'm still trying to be upbeat like Becky, but the whole thing is wearing thin. It's hard to be constantly cheerful and I'm tired. I ask Silva if he sent me a joke message but he says he doesn't know what I'm talking about. I don't believe him but let it go. Then my mobile buzzes and I jump like I've been stung, but it's only a message from Mum. Since she left, she texts me every day.

COME 2 MINE FOR TEA? HAVE DOUGHNUTS x

I text back

AM TOO BUSY.

That was NOT Becky-like, but I can't handle seeing Mum in her new place just yet. It doesn't seem real. And I'm still angry with her. How could she abandon us? Who did she expect would take care of Grandad? Most of her stuff is still at home. She only took a couple of suitcases with her the night she left, but I suppose she was in a hurry. She's desperate for me to move in with her but there's no way I'm leaving my home to sleep on Jez's sofa. I push Mum from my mind.

We're hanging out on the bench outside the shops when Shane Buckerell turns up. He says that he'd texted his sister, Nell, who works in the school kitchens, and found out that the place was crawling with cockroaches.

"There were bugs pouring out of the ceiling in the staffroom," he says, his eyes blazing. "They came swarming out of the drains in the showers and they were in all the biology cupboards. Apparently the floor of the boiler room is five inches deep. Dayo went down to turn down the heating and he heard this cracking, popping noise under his feet, something crunched, he said it was like walking on a box of cornflakes and when he looks down there's all these horrible big bugs crawling up his trousers. It's like an invasion," says Shane.

"Cool," says Silva. "We always knew the place was a dump."

"Nell says that there must have been loads of eggs laid over the last autumn in the school, and because the heating went wrong, it got so warm that they all hatched out at once, and came pouring out, looking for food." Shane shudders. "Yesterday, I ate canteen cooked food. No wonder I had gut rot this morning." He sees a couple of kids from our class across the street and runs off to fill them in.

I knew it must be the bugs. How gross. Silva gets a text. He reads it and grins. Sure enough, he's fixed up a date with Melissa. They're going to the cinema, for the matinee.

"Want to come?" he asks. I shake my head. I need to get back to see Grandad. I bet no one has got him dressed yet. And Dad can't be relied upon to remember the old man's lunch. Anyway, I don't want to be a gooseberry. How does Silva do it? How did he get Melissa's number, and more importantly, how did he get the nerve to ask her out? I couldn't do it in a million years.

"What if she'd said no?" I ask him.

Silva looks puzzled. "What?"

"Wouldn't you die of shame?"

"Of course not. I'd just move on. And women are always nicer to you when they know you fancy them. It increases your chances with them in the future." He gives me a pat on the shoulder. "You've got to be brave, Scrappy boy, if you want to get on with the ladies. You've got to be a love soldier. . ." Silva has this sleepy, relaxed way of talking; he tilts his head back and looks at you through half closed eyes.

"You need to amass your weapons of charm and seduction. Then pound them with your heavy artillery of wit and intelligence." He grins. "It works for me."

I yawn and stretch out my legs. "I'm not a fighting man."

Silva looks at me appraisingly as he rips open a bag of crisps. "You've got the basic toolkit, Scrapper. You've got looks, height, a smattering of intelligence. Now you just need the bravado."

"And how do I get that?" I ask.

Silva sighs. "I dunno. Maybe you need a victory or two under your belt. What's the target? Got anyone in mind?"

I think of Frances Hooper. Her slow smile.

"Nobody," I say.

"Huh." Silva stands and brushes off his trousers. "Every man has a target." He smirks. "Or two or three." He offers me a crisp. "Eat these, they're chilli flavour. They might grow you some balls."

He salutes and flies off in the direction of the Odeon before I can punch him.

And me, I sit on the gum-pocked bench, wondering if I'll ever be brave enough to ask out Frances Hooper. But I know she's out of my league.

My phone buzzes. I've got a text message. I expect it's Sheeley; she's always wanting me to bring her home chocolate or something. I look at the screen. It's not from Sheeley. It's another withheld number. I press the button and read the message. My skin crawls as I read it. It's bizarre.

It's another anonymous dare. And this time, I'm going to do it.

New Mission

U USELESS. U FAILED. NU MSSION: GET CCKROACH FRM
SCHL. SND 2 PO BOX 367 EX12 WJD. RWRD: £50

*F*act. Cockroaches have a fantastically high tolerance
to radiation. If there was a nuclear war and all the
humans were wiped out, then cockroaches could
inherit the earth. Another fact: a female cockroach only
has to be impregnated once in her lifetime to lay about
three hundred eggs. Like me, they prefer warm dark
places and they like food. I can see why they have
earned their reputation as a truly revolting insect. I don't
want to set foot in school again. The internet says you
should keep your premises clean because no amount of
insecticide will eradicate these beasts if there is a
permanent food source. And our school is filthy.

I take a break from the screen and examine my
situation. There's Silva out at the cinema with his new
girl, and here's me at home researching this horrible
bug. I'm such a loser. I flip over my mobile and reread
the most recent text. It has to be from Silva. I got the
message just as he walked off. Could I do it? Should I

play along just for the hell of it? Why not? I'm a bit surprised about the cash part. Silva is usually skint. But I've got nothing else to do apart from looking after Grandad. I'll show Silva who hasn't got any balls. And if on the million-to-one chance this message is the work of some weirdo, well, I'm nearly sixteen and the last time I was measured I was five feet ten. I'm a match for anyone. The only really scary part of this challenge is that I'm going to have to find a way into school, after hours. But there are loads of strangers wandering round my school these days; officials and builders and blokes measuring things and taking photographs, all intent on destroying it, so who knows? There might be an opportunity for me to get in tonight.

Looks like I'm not being a Becky any more.

The bottom door opens and I hear Dad plod up the stairs. He walks like he's on his way to his hanging: slow and sad. Sometimes he bounds up like he's won the lottery. Like I said, I never know what I'm going to get with Dad. Even when he's in a good mood there's an edge to him. He ought to be in a good mood today because Olly said they'd sold over five hundred quid's worth of parts and Shane Buckerell's mum wants to buy the broken camper so she can keep chickens in it.

Dad goes straight to the bathroom and within seconds the shower is thundering. Dad usually has two showers a day. I assume he's in there trying to scrub away the oil and grime from the yard. It doesn't work; his fingers always have oil trapped in the whorls. Dad once said he likes how the noise of the water drowns out everything (i.e., us). Mum always says he's washing away his guilty conscience. I assume she's joking but I do wonder.

About five years ago, Dad vanished. It was a normal school day. Mum still lived here, of course, and Grandad was still helping out in the yard. Anyway, I remember coming home from school and Dad wasn't in his office or in the yard. It struck me as odd because his pickup was parked in its usual place. Sheeley wasn't too bothered so I forgot about it until Mum came home. But she had no idea where he was.

We didn't see him for five weeks. Mum got the police involved and everything. And then, one day, there was Dad, back in his chair and tugging his fingers through his tangled ponytail like always. He never told us where he'd been, and Mum didn't explain either. There's some kind of secret they won't tell me about. My theory is that there was some problem with money for the yard, but I can't be sure. Sheeley was as worried as hell at the time, but after he came back she just seemed to get on with things.

Since then, I've never felt I could trust Dad. I felt like he could abandon us again at any minute. I got that wrong. It's Mum who has gone. Only she's not going to come back.

I change out of my school clothes into my black jeans and a black jumper. This is my camouflage. At the bottom of my drawer I spy a black bomber jacket.

Sheeley gave it to me at Christmas but I've never worn it. It wasn't me. Now I pull it on. It still smells new. I look at my reflection in my mirror and decide to keep it on. Who am I now? I pull my black beanie low over my head and go to hover outside the bathroom door.

I clear my throat. "I'm going to see a mate. I've left Grandad a sandwich, but his toilet is blocked again. . ."

"WHAT?" Even through the drumming water I can hear the annoyance in his voice.

"GOING TO THE . . . never mind."

I leave him a note instead and head out. Look at me; I'll do anything to get out of the house. It's dark out, and wet. Petal hears me splashing through the puddles and starts barking as wildly as if a giant pussycat was about to steal her dinner. I walk through the lamplit yard, round the office cabin to the back car park. The old aeroplane sits in the gloom, rain dribbling down the glass. I climb the stepladder, wrench open the door and clamber in, fumbling for my torch. I savour the familiar smells of oil, dust and old rubber. I step into the cockpit. Just for a minute I am transported into the sky, tearing up clouds and travelling at five hundred miles an hour. I fumble around until my fingers close on a box of matches. I shake out the contents and stuff the empty box into my pocket. I step outside and close the flight door with a loud creak.

When I'm finally pedalling down the lane, I can feel my heart thumping. I'm thinking of phoning Silva and letting him know what I'm doing. I can't feel my phone in my pocket. I must have left it at home. After this I might set up a dare for Silva. What would I make him do? Eat five cans of baked beans? No, that's too tame. I'm capable of thinking up something much more twisted.

I blend into the roundabout and concentrate on not getting mashed by the tired and angry traffic leaving the motorway.

I padlock my bike to the railings outside the school and the rain squalls around me as I creep through the gates. Then I flatten myself into the hedge as a white PESTAWAY van pulls out of the car park. I unstick myself from the leaves and slink down the driveway, ready to bolt.

I'm buzzing. At last something is happening in my life, even if I'm not sure what it is. I guess I'm doing this to prove something to Silva, or maybe to prove something to myself.

The school is in darkness. There used to be lots of evening classes and things going on (Mum went to keep fit every Wednesday, Silva's dad was learning Italian) but now there's only one PESTAWAY van parked here. It's so quiet I can hear the swollen river rushing behind the playing fields. To the far right I can see a dim glow coming from the old shot tower by the river. Apparently the tower was used to make lead shot. They'd drop boiling gobbets of lead from the top and when it hit the freezing water at the bottom it would be frozen into the perfect shape. It's disused now and looks derelict.

The lights flicker on the top floor of the humanities block and I see a shadow move past the window. The school looks bigger and meaner at night. It's odd that soon it won't exist. It really must be crap. We are the last generation of students to come out of a crap school. It doesn't feel good.

I decide to try the gym. Sometimes the windows get left open. The wet from the grass in the playing field soaks through my shoes and I can barely see a thing. The lights from the town shine in the distance but this doesn't prevent me slipping in a muddy patch and sprawling over. I scan the wall of the gym. No windows have been left open. Feeling like a career criminal, I try the door, but it doesn't budge. If this was a book or a film, it would be unlocked, I'd creep into the gym and would find a pack of flesh-eating zombies, and I'd have to zap them all with my doubledeath blaster.

I sneak around the back of the school, trying every door, but they're all locked. I look through the window of the languages huts and swear I can see something moving over the floor. I bet it's a cockroach. Only I can't get in and I'm not about to break a window. I'm not that desperate. I'm only going to do this if it is easy. Then I see that the door to the humanities block is standing wide open.

Technically I'm not breaking in. I'm just walking through an open door. I stand on the brightly lit threshold, take a deep breath and step into the corridor, looking left to right. The floor is coated with a fine white dust. It must be the stuff they've been putting down. Where the hell am I going to find a cockroach? I remember my research. They like warmth and dark and food.

There is a year seven common room just along the corridor. It's been empty since all the younger kids left. It has a small tuck shop in a corner cupboard. I can't imagine the cleaners have gone insane cleaning it out when it is going to be demolished in a few months. The door into the common room is ajar and I make my way inside, propping the door open so the light from the corridor floods the room. I search the floors, the walls and the ceiling but nothing moves. I look under cracks in the walls and gingerly feel under the tuck cupboard door. My fingertips touch something small and papery and I want to retch. Carefully I ease out an insect trap. Inside are two dead roaches. Now I do gag. The insects are bigger than the one I saw this morning; they have nasty feelers and shiny armoured backs. I pick them up in a tissue and hold them at arm's length. I drop them into my matchbox. Then feel a burning in my throat and start coughing.

Then it hits me. How could I have been so stupid? They're putting down chemicals to kill the cockroaches, and to kill a creature that can survive a radiation blast, the chemicals must be very powerful. I stumble into the corridor and out of the building. I look up at the second floor window and see a white-suited figure emptying stuff out of a bottle. He has a black mask on his face like Darth Vader. I scuttle off, behind a tree, gasping deep breaths of the wet night air. Have I set a small and deadly fleck of poison in motion inside me? What damage will it do?

I've retrieved my bike and am wheeling it towards the gates when I hear voices. I crouch behind the nearest solid object, which happens to be the PESTAWAY van. As I try to slow my breathing I see two figures materialize from the gloom, walking down the pavement outside school. I see the red glow of a cigarette and hear muffled laughter. I'd recognize that sound anywhere. It's Judge, and he's with his mate Louis. My stomach tightens. This is big trouble. I make myself as still as I can, willing them not to see me. This may be a coincidence. Judge only lives a couple of streets away. But what if this whole thing is a set-up and the message was from Judge and not Silva at all?

What if I'm next on Judge's hit list?

Dad

The two floodlit shadows pass the other side of the van. I don't know if they've seen me. Why are they in school if they're not intending to get me? I run through the last few days, trying to think of anything I might have done to get on the wrong side of Judge. But there's nothing – at least, nothing recent. Is it possible that they haven't seen me, or are they just bluffing? Any second I expect to get dragged out and humiliated. But now they're walking away down the road so I may be OK after all. All the same, I'm not going to advertise the fact I'm here, alone. Shane Buckerell was Judge's victim way back in year eight, and I swear it nearly killed him. I don't know why but Judge initiated a whispering campaign against him. Rumours, like head lice, spread quickly and easily in school, and they're just as hard to get rid of.

He was hit on his head with a hammer as a baby.

He's lost part of his skull; now his brain has grown too big and is pressurized.

He might explode and go mad.

He has to pop pills to keep him sane.

Don't be alone with him, he's secretly violent.

Once people think you are mad, it's difficult to prove them wrong. Everything you do can be interpreted as the act of a madman.

Why do you think he's always coming out with stupid stories?

Why does he have to wear glasses? (The pressure in his head has affected his eyesight.)

Why does he never, never have an ironed shirt? (Because he can't have an iron in his house, the smell of hot metal drives him crazy.)

Not everyone believed all this stuff, of course, and the rumours died down. But Shane has been tainted. Nobody knows any more what is real and what is not. No one is completely sure about him. They did the same to a girl in my class, Sarah Blue, last year. The rumour went round that she was born with six toes on each foot and her parents got the extra ones lopped off at birth. You can't help but wonder if it's true. So that's Judge's speciality: making up lies about people; nasty lies that stain. But that's not his only trick. He's inventive. He gets a kick out of making people feel like crap. Me and Silva go out of our way to avoid him. But now I don't know what to think. Has he got it in for me, or not?

I've got half a mind to go straight round to Silva's now, confront him with the bug and see what he says. But it's getting late and I'm tired and wet. I'll send it by post as per the instructions.

I'm pedalling out into the street when a large figure

materializes from the gloom. I hear a muffled cough. I'd recognize that sound anywhere.

"Scrappy, is that you?"

Dear Lord, it's my old man. There's no time to hide as he strides up. He looks massive. Despite everything, I hope I don't turn out like him: heavy and sweating and out of breath.

"Scrappy," he says. "Michael." He grabs hold of my handlebars like he's worried I'm going to pedal off.

"What are you doing here?" I stutter. I don't know what to think. Why's he here?

"Looking for you," says Dad. In the lamplight he looks tired and worried. "You haven't done anything stupid, have you?"

I'm too surprised to say anything.

"I'll come clean," says Dad. "I found your phone. I read your text. I was worried."

I blink, my confusion turning to rage.

"I'm sorry," says Dad. "Only I didn't know where you'd gone. . ."

"Since when did you give a monkey's where I am?" I growl. This is insane. Dad has barely said a word to me for ages. Now he's acting like the concerned dad and reading my texts.

"I don't want you getting into trouble, Scrappy," says Dad. "All that stuff about cockroaches. Look, I don't want to have this conversation in the street. I'll give you a lift home." In a daze I follow Dad back to his truck, which is parked just round the corner. I'm so angry I can't say a word to him. How dare he read my texts. How *dare* he?

"Let's stop at the chippy on the way back," says Dad, chucking my bike in the back. "I expect you're hungry. We'll get Ted a sausage."

"You read my texts," I growl.

Dad sighs. "You didn't break into school, did you?"

"Why are you so bothered all of a sudden?" I snap. I don't usually talk to Dad like this. It's too risky. He has a short temper and can't stand it if me or Sheeley cheek him, but right now, I'm really mad.

Dad clears his throat. "I'm sorry," he says. "And I was out of order with Ted," he says. "I lost the plot, didn't I? But I don't know what to do. He's out of control."

Whatever I say will be wrong. It's best not to say anything. We arrive at the chippy and Dad pulls over. He switches off the engine and looks at me. Even in the gloom I can see the lines etched in his pale, stubbly, heavy face. He's aged recently.

"I looked at your messages because I thought there might be something from your mum," he says in a quiet, humble sort of voice. "I wasn't checking up on you. That's how I saw the stuff about the cockroach. It's a dare, isn't it? Who's it from?"

I shrug. This apologetic Dad is freaking me out. I wish he'd just leave me alone, like usual.

"I miss her, Michael," says Dad, his fingers clenching the steering wheel. "I miss her like mad." He gets out of the car. "Coming?"

I shake my head. I'd rather wait in the car.

I watch Dad walk his big mass into the shop. He bangs his shoulder clumsily on the door frame. I suppose I can just about understand why he read my texts. I miss Mum too. Maybe if he'd have been a bit nicer to her she'd have stuck around. But what kills me about Dad is that one minute he's like this, acting all concerned; the next, he's shut away in his office and will chew my head off if I ask him if he wants a cup of tea. It does my nut in. It did Mum's nut in too. She was always trying to keep him happy, and I'd back her up. I think we only end up irritating him.

I remember this time when I was little. It was Dad's birthday. Mum went to loads of trouble making him this cake she'd seen in a magazine. She had to start again because the cream curdled or something. Anyway, eventually she finished it, and got balloons and candles from somewhere, and wrapped him up a new shirt. Me and Sheeley watched the preparations, bemused. Dad has never been one to make a song and dance about birthdays, least of all his own.

That afternoon, she took it down to him in the garage and made us come with her. Dad was standing in his dirty blue overalls, his hair tied back with an elastic band and a smudge of oil on his face. He was scribbling on a clipboard, trying to get his biro working. Mum made us sing "Happy Birthday" as she put the big yellow cake on his workbench. Then we waited. This is the bit that gets me. You see, none of us knew how he'd react. And Mum stood behind us, clamping the birthday shirt in her armpit. I remember her hand pressing heavier on my shoulder.

Then Dad said, "You're all gorgeous."

And he put down his clipboard, and cut each of us a slice of cake with his penknife. And we wagged our tails and shone like the moon.

When we get home, Dad mutters about checking something in the office and I head straight to my room. Sheeley is sitting in the hallway on the telephone, twisting her silver ring around her finger. It's less expensive to use the landline than her mobile. She's obsessed with saving money so she can raise her rotten deposit.

"Where've you been?" she mouths. "Mum called."

I shrug. I'm not going to tell her. Sheeley leans back and resumes her telephone conversation.

I lock my door and place the roaches on the high shelf, as far away from the bed as possible, which isn't far in my tiny room. Then I go out to put Grandad to bed.

I wake early. This is annoying because there's no school to get up for. I try to get back to sleep but the flat is too noisy. I hear the bog flushing and the telly blathering. I put my pillow over my head until I get too hot and have to throw it off. I give up on sleep and switch on the light. I immediately notice the matchbox lying open on the floor. How did that happen? I could have trodden on it. There's only one small, cockroach corpse left inside. I scan the carpet and turn over books, but can't see the other one anywhere. They were both dead, I'm sure of it, but where could it have gone? I look under the bed, on the shelf, everywhere, but there's no sign of the thing. It's vanished. It's probably burrowed into one of my books. I don't like to think of it alive and scurrying around. I open the curtains. It's still dark outside but amazingly, it's not raining, not even a drizzle. There's a light on in the office. Dad is slumped over the desk, his head in his arms. He gets worked up about money, goes out to do some late-night office business and ends up falling asleep. It almost seems like Dad will spend the night anywhere except in his bed. Even now, with Mum gone, he won't sleep in it.

I stand by the mirror, my morning ritual. Today I don't feel light and cheerful. Today I just feel mean. I pull off the wristband. Today, naturally, I will wear black. I'm going to be like Judge; big and nasty and powerful. I'll see what happens.

The first thing I do when I get up is cycle out to the postbox at the service station and mail the cockroach. I'll play along with Silva, just for now. He's pretty ingenious, though, what with setting up his own PO box address and all. But that's Silva all over. He's always up to something. On my way back I stop at the bridge. I lean on it and watch the traffic.

When Sheeley and I were little, Grandad told us that

you never ever walk by the motorway because the cars cause a strong air current that could easily suck a little kid up and throw them right into the traffic. That's why, he said, you'd see birds struggling to stay airborne above the lanes. Grandad also told us about the Geebos. These are ghost people who have died in car crashes who float up and down the motorway all day long, looking for trouble. They're like the poltergeists of the road. They grab steering wheels and spin them round and they can make drivers temporarily blind. Geebos, says Grandad, are responsible for over half of all fatal accidents. Of course I don't believe any of that stuff.

I hear a familiar racket as an air horn blares out its raucous tune. Sheeley whizzes past me in her mini. Then she brakes, causing the Golf behind to screech its brakes and honk like mad.

"Skiver, why aren't you in school?" she yells, sticking her head out of her window.

"Cockroach infestation," I call. "You nearly caused an accident."

"Did I?" Sheeley looks surprised. "How?"

"By being a crap driver."

"You're just jealous, Mr Pedal Power. Oh, I haven't seen Grandad yet this morning. Now get off the roads before I mow you down." She circles the roundabout and drives off to town.

Then I hear a loud, loud engine and I watch an Audi sports car fly up in the fast lane below. It's hanging on the tail of the car in front, way too close. It must be going at least a hundred miles an hour. I watch as the other cars slow and pull in and the Audi soars past. He flies over the road and lingers on the horizon, an angry black dot, before he vanishes. I think bad thoughts about him; maybe I'm jealous. I'd love a car like that, one day.

Then there is an almighty crashing noise, a noise of grinding metal and hard things smashing into each other. The noise seems to echo under the bridge. I freeze and wait and watch, and slowly a plume of black smoke rises over the ridge. The traffic is already slowing. I wait, my heart thumping. Should I call 999? I can't see what's happened. I wait a few minutes as the traffic comes to a standstill below me; then from far away I hear the whine of emergency vehicles. This looks serious. I watch as three police cars and an ambulance hurtle down the hard shoulder. Somewhere, not far away, someone's day has gone badly wrong.

Geebo

I'm transfixed. I'm just studying the roofs and bonnets idling below. If these people had set out just a few minutes earlier, they would have been caught up in the smash. If Sheeley had decided to go up to Exeter for the day, instead of into town, she too would have been involved. The engines roar and purr and sputter, belching out grey fumes. A fire engine appears, screaming and flashing, zooming along the hard shoulder and towards the mayhem. It makes me feel sick but I can't tear myself away. After ages, the traffic begins to inch forward in one lane. I breathe deeply and am climbing on my bike, my legs feeling all shaky, when a tow truck tears round the corner. Olly puts his thumb up and grins at me, flashing his big yellow teeth.

"Coming?" he yells.

"No," I shout. "No bloody way." I'm not sick like that. Olly laughs and flies down the slip road on to the hard shoulder. Only a good serious crash makes Olly smile. A few seconds later, he's followed by Dad in his pickup. Dad doesn't bother to wave. He hates accidents, which is a bit of a problem when you consider his job.

When I get back the lights are still blazing in the yard. I make some toast and coffee and carry it out to Grandad's cottage. His front door is yawning open. I hope he hasn't done another runner. But when I walk in his stinking hallway I hear the telly blasting away from the sitting room and see Grandad, asleep on the sofa. I'm supposed to be a hard man today, and no hard man does housework, but Grandad's place is disgusting. I clear the side table and put the toast down. I go into the kitchen and dig a plastic bag out from under the sink. Then I start chucking away the worst stuff: used tissues, newspapers, food cans, filthy dishcloths. Every time I come round here, it's like Grandad can do less and less for himself. I chuck all the washing up in another bin bag and put it outside. I'll get Sheeley to do it in the flat. Then I pick up three cat turds in a tissue, open the window and fling them out. No one goes in the garden any more so it doesn't matter.

I can't stop thinking about the crash. The noise keeps replaying in my head, the sound of breaking metal. I can't help thinking, in a mad sort of way, that if I hadn't been standing there, watching the traffic, the accident wouldn't have happened.

I check to see if Grandad has woken up and find Jasper on the side table, eating the toast.

"Get out, you furry demon." I grab him by his scruff and drop him to the floor.

Grandad opens one bleary eye. "Where's my

breakfast?" he asks. As he shifts in the chair I get a strong waft of urine. It could come from the cat or Grandad, or both.

"Morning, Grandad," I say. I can't disguise the irritation in my voice. I do so much for him, and he just bitches at me.

"I'm hungry," says Grandad, blinking. "Bloody kids."

"The cat ate your toast; I'll get you some more."

"Not Sheeley," says Grandad. "Bossy little madam."

On my way out, I remember who I'm supposed to be today. I'm Judge. I'm mean and powerful. I like being Judge. So, just for the hell of it, I quietly remove all of Grandad's faded aeroplane pictures from the hall on the wall and lay them neatly next to each other, making a path in the hallway. He's got about twelve pictures. I never really looked at them before, but each one depicts a different type of early light aircraft.

"HELL," Grandad moans, from his chair, talking to himself. "Where's that BOY with my BREAKFAST?"

In a surge of anger I step on each picture as I leave, the glass cracking satisfyingly under my shoes.

As I go back to the flat, carrying the two bin bags, it occurs to me that it would be easier looking after Grandad if he was a nice old man. The sort who would tell me cool stuff, ask me about things, thank me for his breakfast. Instead he's foul-mouthed and incontinent. That's why none of us like going to see him. The only time I enjoy his company is when we're playing around with the plane, but that hasn't happened for ages. But it can't carry on like this. Dad has to do something. I wish I'd said something to him last night.

I make another round of toast, chuck on a couple of bags of crisps for Grandad's lunch and haul my ass all the way back to the old cottage.

Amazingly, Grandad has changed his trousers by the time I get back. He's standing in his hallway, gazing stupidly at the broken pictures. His coffee is soaking into the carpet by his feet where he has dropped his mug.

"Look," he breathes, pointing.

I arrange my face into an expression of shock. "It must have been the Geebos, Grandad. There's been a big crash today. They must have come up here."

"What?" Grandad looks at me with such horror in his old eyes that I ought to feel ashamed. But I don't feel anything. I pick up the pictures, roughly hanging them, one by one. Mostly the glass is just cracked but there are shards glinting here and there.

"We're going to see some action in the yard," I tell him. "Dad and Olly have gone out with the trucks. It was a big accident." I fetch the dustpan and brush and sweep up the broken glass.

"I'll be up after my breakfast," says Grandad. "I don't want to be alone here this morning, not after this." He gazes at his pictures.

I've done it now, haven't I? Dad hates Grandad hanging round the yard but he can hardly stop him. Grandad still owns the place, on paper anyway.

"Your grandmother gave me those pictures," says Grandad. "She gave me a new one every birthday."

"We can get them fixed," I say, wondering if I am a monster.

"No point," says Grandad. "The Geebos will only do it again."

I don't know what to say so I leave him to his banquet of cold toast. Grandad is a superstitious old man. He'll be on about this for ever. I go and wait in the office and try to put the incident out of my mind. It wasn't me, after all. It was Judge.

The office sounds grand but really it is just a converted shipping container (I like to think it once brought a brand new car over the ocean). A door and a couple of windows have been cut out of the sides. Dad's got a desk, a phone, a couple of chairs, and an ancient PC sitting on a rickety old table. A greasy old sofa is wedged against the back wall. Dad sleeps on that. The place stinks of oil and sweat and the floor is grimy with mouse droppings.

The first car to arrive is a lemon-yellow Lexus. The bonnet is all crumpled up. Olly dumps it out front in the holding bay. He turns round and sets off again before I have a chance to ask him about the crash. The holding bay is the place where new wrecks are brought in, and some stay there until the insurance claims are sorted out. Then the cars are dragged to the big yard, where they are picked over by Olly and my dad and on a Saturday morning, me. We're like a team of ants, stripping everything that is salvageable, like stereos, CDs, carpet mats and engine parts, lights. We can get loads out of wrecks, depending on age. Sheeley says we are like organ transplant surgeons. Both professions rely on a good supply of organs from roadkill to supply our trade. Depending on the type of car, eventually, when there's nothing left but the body, it gets crushed as small as possible, and every so often a huge lorry comes and takes them away. Then they get shipped overseas to be recycled.

Shortly after the Lexus, Dad arrives with a mangled Fiat on the back of his truck. He tells me there was a pile-up on the motorway, northbound, between our junction and the next one. Apparently eleven cars were involved. I think of the noise, the smoke and the heat. Cars are the most dangerous things I know.

Olly's truck rumbles back into the yard. His bright lights are blinding. He grins out of the window, his grey sideburns sticking out like wire. He's brought us an Audi, a newish one. I get a wave of sickness as I recognize it from earlier. The car is only three years old, and as it has been brought here, it must be a total write-off. At first glance it doesn't look so bad. Olly switches off his engine and I hear music. Freakily, the radio is still playing in the wreck. Then I see the back. The whole boot has come off, been torn away neatly. Dad whistles when he sees it. He's impressed. It takes a lot to impress my dad. I should know.

I dread to think what has happened to the driver. I

see something like that and I think there should be a law, forcing people to drive slower, to go no more than forty miles an hour and to retake their driving test at least every ten years. The radio is loud, playing some retro tune. Sometimes wiring melts and fuses together, creating pathways and making things work which should be silent and dead, like an auto Frankenstein's monster.

"Turn that thing off," Dad snaps at Olly.

"You do it," says Olly, and stamps off into the garage.

Dad sighs. Like Grandad, Olly's superstitious when it comes to wrecks. He won't touch them if he thinks someone has died in them.

We get eight wrecks in that morning. Some are worse than others. I'm busy helping Dad fill out some of the basic paperwork. Dad's totally disorganized. All his bills and invoices, receipts and car documents are in a mess. Mum used to do all that stuff but she stopped when she got her job at the youth hostel. I quite enjoy sorting stuff into piles and putting things in the right folder. On mornings like these I can feel almost happy.

There's a quiet bit halfway through the day, when Olly's gone home for lunch and Dad goes to do some work in the flat. (We haven't got internet in the office.) When he's gone I go for a poke around the new cars. I'm drawn to that Audi. I peer inside the windscreen and do a double take. There's an enormous insect on the driver's seat. It looks like a huge brown wasp and is as big as my thumb. But it has no stripes, so it can't be a wasp. It crawls over the seat towards me, its wings whirring on its back. It has huge orange bulbous eyes and antennae with revolting red specks on the end. It is the most horrible thing I have ever seen. I stare transfixed as it creeps towards me. Without warning it takes off and fires straight at me, emitting a loud low buzz that makes the hairs on the back of my neck stand on end. There's a dull thud as it thwacks into the windscreen and I shriek like a girl and topple backwards and fall on my arse. I get up and flinch as the thing slams into the windscreen again, only lower down, like it's trying to get me.

I pelt back into the office and slam the door.

What an evil-looking thing. It's like a bug from another country, something you might expect to see in the jungle. When I've calmed down a bit I try to reason with myself. Imagine being scared of a bug! But the size of it! I grab an old newspaper to while away the time until Dad gets back. But I'm freaked out and I keep thinking I can hear a buzzing noise in my ears. I'm reading the football pages when I hear a tapping on the window. I stand up so quickly my chair falls over. The massive bug slams against the glass, again and again. It's terrifying. How did it get out of the car? What is it with me and insects at the moment? The bug flies all over the window, like it's seeking a way in. Then it vanishes and I am left staring at the grey sky, but before I can relax the buzzing starts up again and the thing appears at the opposite window, hammering the glass. Oh my god, it really is after me. What is it about me? Is it the way I'm dressed? But I'm wearing grey; I don't remotely resemble a flower. Maybe it's the way I smell. My teenage pheromones are driving it wild. I hold out for a few more minutes before I pick up the phone and call the flat. Dad doesn't pick up for ages.

"Yes?" he speaks in his gruff voice.

"Dad, it's me. There's a horrible great big insect, a hornet or something chasing me. It flew out of the Audi. It wants to get me." My voice is high-pitched and squeaky.

"What?" Dad sounds exasperated

"This horrible BUG, Dad, I swear it's come from another country. I've never seen anything like it. It's slapping into the window. Have we got any spray? I'm a prisoner in here." There is a long silence during which I hear Dad breathe in and out three or four times. "Dad?"

Finally he speaks. "Michael, I'm having one hell of a morning. One of the cars brought in this morning looks like it has been stolen. The number plate is cooked. I've got to sort it out. Understand? And you're telling me you can't deal with a wasp? What's the matter with you? Swat it with a newspaper." He rings off. I look at the receiver and feel myself shrinking a little. I check the windows and the insect isn't there. I wait for a minute or so before I go to the door. But as I open it I get a start of fear; a flash of orange hurtles itself at me. It's going to land on my face. I gape in terror but before I have a chance to move, something smashes it away. Here's Grandad, sprung from nowhere. He's only gone and flattened the bug against the office wall with his bare hand.

"Jesus, Grandad, did it sting you?"

Grandad looks a little dazed as he examines his fist. The dead hornet is smeared on the metal wall. Its antennae still seem to be moving but it's dead all right.

"It was going for you," says Grandad. He leans against the wall. "I saw it going for you, Michael." We look at the hideous, mutilated body. Then Grandad sighs and I see all this excitement has been too much for him and I help him into a chair in the office.

"It looked like it belongs in a zoo," I joke weakly.

"It belongs in hell," says Grandad.

And when I go back outside the thing has fallen off the wall, leaving only a smear, and is lying half buried in the mud, one orange eye still intact, beaming up evils from the ground. I move the flowerpot over it. I never want to see it again.

"Has it gone?" calls Grandad.

"Yeah," I say. "I buried it."

Grandad comes outside.

"You can never get rid of a Geebo," he says. "Not once it's fixed on you. That's the second time it has bothered us today."

"Grandad, Geebos do not exist," I tell him.

"What was that then?" asks Grandad. "And what

about my pictures?" But we both fall silent as Dad comes out of the flat and over the yard.

"Hope you've not been messing with the paperwork, Ted," growls Dad.

"I've got every right. . ." begins Grandad, but I grab his arm.

"Come and look at these cars, Grandad," I say. "See what you think." There are have been some epic battles between these two and I don't want to be in the middle of another one. Grandad allows me to lead him off. But not before he's said his parting speech.

"It's no place for a kid to grow up, Thomas, especially now Catherine's gone. Thomas?"

But Dad slams the door in his face.

Plane

After lunch, I'm lying on my bed, reading, when I get a text from Silva asking if I want to go over to his. I reply immediately.

DFINATLY. MGHT BRNG MY SUITCSE WIV ME!

I'm out of here. If I spend much longer with these madmen I might turn into one. I'm not being a depraved Judge any more; the novelty has worn off. I look in the mirror and wonder how to present myself. I'm not being a sunny Becky. I don't want to skitter around like Mum, and I'm not feeling arsey like Sheeley, or sharp like Silva. For now, I feel like being myself.

Silva lives on the other side of town. His house is off a quiet lane, fringed with trees. It's a proper house with a driveway, a garage, front and back gardens and three floors. It's also pretty old. I hope to live in a house like Silva's one day even though it's quite knackered. Outside, the paint is faded, some of the glass in the windows is cracked and the garden looks like a nature reserve. Becky, Silva's mum, is just driving off in her Fiesta as I arrive. She winds down the window.

"Hello, stranger," she calls. "I've got to dash, but the door is open. See you very soon." Becky is thin with very short hair and a smiley open face. She wears dangly earrings and brightly coloured skirts. She's supposed to be the daughter of some famous politician or other. She once said I was her honorary son, which was nice. I listen as her car accelerates down the street.

I climb the steps, say hello to the ugly lion door knocker and let myself in. I pass through the entrance hall and step into the kitchen. When I first came here, about five years ago, I was freaked out by the mess. The Moxley house is like one big junk shop. Vases of dead flowers drop brown petals on surfaces already swimming with upended greetings cards, unopened bills, and all kinds of tat. Books are piled up on the floor next to a chewed dog basket and the big dangling light shades are draped with cobwebs and mottled with fly poo. The kitchen has a big cast-iron stove which burns logs all winter, and is laden with drying washing, food debris and a half-eaten pan of stew. The floor is old cracked slate and is covered with faded rugs which wriggle across the ground throughout the day. Silva is one of six children. He is in the middle, age wise, with two older sisters (one of whom is mates with Sheeley) and three younger brothers. The youngest brother is six years old and the eldest girl is nineteen, so the whole house is littered with papers and homework and toys and batteries and handbags and shoes and more shoes and coats and scarves. Silva's parents are hippies. There's no polite way of saying it. Silva's dad is an artist. His paintings are all over the walls. The twisted rainbow images are supposed to represent inner feelings, or so Silva says. Silva's dad, Kennett (I asked Silva if that was his real name, and Silva said he was sixty per cent sure it wasn't), has a big studio next to Silva's bedroom in the attic. Sometimes he lets us in there and shows us his latest painting and we pretend to love it. He'll chat on about stuff, the news, or something he's read, or something one of his kids has been up to. At these times Silva will roll his eyes at me, but I think Kennett's quite cool. He got me into reading fiction and lends me loads of books. I don't know if my dad has ever read a book in his life. Kennett's room has got big skylights and a kind of round window in the roof to look up at the rain clouds.

I pass Rio and Bligh, Silva's small brothers. They're playing computer games in the corner of the kitchen and take no notice of me. His sister Millie is reading on the window seat. She's a year older than me and quite fit, though I'd never tell Silva that. Millie nods at me.

"He's upstairs."

So I climb up to the very top of the house, passing walls plastered with painting, school photos and crayon scribbles. Silva's bedroom is a sloping attic. In summer it feels like you are nesting in the trees with birds swaying on branches just outside the window. I knock on the door and Silva opens it. His room has bare floorboards which creak when you walk over them. He's got bunk beds and a desk and computer. He's got three guitars hanging from hooks on the walls and a lime green electric one lying on the floor. A massive amplifier sits against one wall. Silva's always swapping and changing his guitars. He's pretty good but gets stage fright so his musical career isn't very promising. He's also got a rotten potato in the corner of his room. He says it's an experiment. He wants to see how long it will be before it completely disappears. Silva's always doing experiments. Like exactly how many times does he have to tap Millie on the foot before she punches him, or which small brother blinks the most, or if his poo goes yellow if he eats five bananas, or if the colour of his mother's skirt corresponds with what sort of food there is in the fridge, that sort of thing. He says he's curious about connections in the universe.

"I did it," I say, referring to the cockroaches.

"Congratulations," he says, unfazed, as he steps aside to let me in. "Whatever it was you did." He kicks some stuff under the bed. I look at him sideways but his hair is hanging over his face and I can't read his expression. Is he serious?

"You'll get it tomorrow," I say. "The job's done."

Silva pulls his hair back into a ponytail and turns to face me. "I'm lost, mate. We're talking total wilderness."

"You didn't send me the message?" I ask, expecting him to crack any minute and come clean.

"What message? Come on, boy, less of the cryptic stuff." Silva puts his head on one side. He looks amused. I'm about to elaborate but then I hesitate. What if Silva really isn't behind my cockroach challenge? The idea makes me feel spooked. If it's not Silva, then who is?

I decide to say nothing more on the subject. I'll let nature take its course. He'll spill the beans sooner or later. Silva's not one for secrets.

"Explain yourself, man," says Silva. "What evil deed are you accusing me of?"

I flop down on to his bed. "Oh, nothing. I've got my wires crossed."

Silva looks sceptical so to throw him off the scent I tell him about the crash and the Audi wasp. In a flash he's booting up his laptop and trawling the web.

"Was that it?" he asks, pointing to the screen. "Was it a Northern European queen hornet?"

"It didn't have a furry bum like that," I reply, studying the horrifying-looking creature on the screen. "And it was browner, and it buzzed like a, I don't know, like machine rather than an animal."

"Maybe it was a machine," says Silva. "A killer nanobot sent to destroy you." He glances at me. "Got any enemies?"

I think of my anonymous messages. "Possibly."

Finally Silva hits on a picture that looks a little like the beast in the Mondeo. *Vespra Mandarina*. It is a giant Asian hornet and its sting can be fatal. "That's it!" I yell. "That's the thing I saw."

"Sorry," huffs Silva. "It can't be."

"But it is," I insist. "It's definitely the same. It's got the same brown body, the orange eyes and the red-tipped antennae. That's the monster that wanted my blood."

"Scraps, you're wrong," says Silva quietly. "This hornet has never been found on the British Isles."

I look closer at the picture. The thing seems to grow larger before my eyes. I duck back as its wings begin to whirr and its body jerks and creeps forward. One leg slowly lifting up, poised.

"Switch it off," I say. "It's freaking me out."

"Ugly-looking bug," says Silva, scrolling down the page. "It says they sometimes attack animals, or even people, with deadly results. Swarms of them killed bee colonies. And when the bees die, that means a hole right at the beginning of the food chain. You know, if one link goes down, so do all the rest. If the plants don't get pollinated, then nothing can grow. If nothing grows then bigger animals, like cows, have nothing to eat, and that means we have nothing to eat."

"Thanks for the biology lecture," I say.

"It's serious, man." Silva swivels round on his chair and looks at me. "If you really have seen one of these things, Scrappy, it's a public health disaster."

I shrug. "It's dead now."

"Good," says Silva and banishes the screen. He swivels round to look at me. "I haven't forgotten about this message business you were on about."

"Nor have I," I say carefully.

We mess around Silva's house for the rest of the day. I love it here. I feel really at home. Silva's family are so chilled. It's a million miles away from my home life. We're in the kitchen playing old CDs when Kennett comes in. He's plastered in paint, even his shoes, with a long smudge of yellow down his cheek, like an old bruise.

"Hey, Scrappy." He nods at me. "I heard your mum moved out. I'm sorry. Are you OK?"

I nod. "It's probably for the best," I mutter, and I realize it is true.

"Where are you going to live?" asks Kennett. "Or is that none of my business?"

"I'm staying put," I say. "Mum's new place is too small."

Kennett nods. "You know, you're always welcome here." He opens the fridge and surveys the contents. "You lads should check out the night sky tomorrow night. If the rain blows over you'll see Venus with the naked eye. Want a sandwich?"

He makes us each a hot bacon roll and a mug of tea. The last time someone made me a meal was over a month ago. Mum made me pie and mash the night she left.

"Venus is the second closest planet to the sun," says Kennet, passing me the sugar. "A wise planet, if you ask me. Hanging with the light."

"Bloody hippy," mutters Silva as his dad vanishes back up to his studio.

I just grin. My dad would never say something like that. On my way home I feel lifted, lighter. Life doesn't seem quite so bad. I'm like a kind of leech that feeds off Silva's family, sucking into their happiness. They don't seem to notice how hungry I am.

I give myself a little shake. I've got to stop thinking crap like this. Sometimes my own thoughts surprise me – I mean, the stuff that comes out of my head! I decide to stop at the supermarket and buy some food. Dad left some money on the kitchen counter. Planning dinners should get my head back on the straight and narrow.

"Michael. MICHAEL! Get up. You're going to be late." I pull my duvet over my head. It's only eight a.m. Sheeley hammers on my door. I sit up and rub my eyes. No more sleep for me. The door handle twists and she stalks in. I hate being invaded like this, first thing in the morning. I haven't looked in the mirror. I haven't done my magic. I don't know who I am yet.

"You've overslept," she says, toning down her voice when she clocks my obviously-just-woken state.

"No, I've underslept," I say. "School is closed. There's a cockroach infestation and they're fumigating the whole place. It was shut yesterday as well. Ring school if you like. There's bound to be a recorded message for disbelievers." The speech has worn me out so I flop back into bed and shut my eyes.

"Are you joking?"

I open one eye. Sheeley is fully dressed and made up, with high-heeled boots and purple-blue eyeshadow. But under all the make-up she looks tired and washed out.

"No," I say. "Can I go back to sleep now?" I hear her breathing, eyeing me up. She's trying to work out if I'm lying.

"Cockroaches?"

"Yep, they spread from the canteen."

Sheeley was late home last night. I was already in bed. I was feeling paranoid, worrying that the missing cockroach was going to scuttle over my face when I was asleep. Every little noise set me on edge. It was way past eleven before I heard her key in the door. Soon she won't be coming home at all.

"Look, Scrappy, Mum really wants to see you. She's worried about you. She says you're not replying to her calls or texts. You haven't seen her for ages." Sheeley sits on the end of my bed. "This is tough for me too, OK? But Mum's better off out of here. You know what she and Dad were like."

I do. This place is too small for people who are afraid of each other.

"Go and see her today," Sheeley orders.

But I'm fed up with being told what to do. "If she cared so much, why has she left me to look after Grandad?" I ask. "I'm a kid, not a social worker."

Sheeley looks a bit sheepish. "We're all responsible for Grandad," she says. "I tell you what. I'll take him his breakfast today."

"Good," I say.

"This was in a bag tied on the front gate." She passes me a brown envelope with my name on it. "What is it?"

"Mind your own business," I say and pull the duvet over my head. I wait until Sheeley leaves before I emerge and tear the envelope open. Inside are five ten-pound notes. I sit up and examine them. For a minute I can't think what they are for; then I remember. It's my reward for the cockroach. For a moment I am elated. But then the demons crawl in. This ups the stakes. Whoever is behind this is serious. Silva is hardly ever serious about anything. I'm beginning to think I'm going to have to eradicate him from my list of suspects. I'm left with Judge and his crew, someone at school, a family member, or an outsider. I rub the notes between finger and thumb. They're crisp and new. It occurs to me that I only posted the cockroach yesterday, so it wouldn't have arrived until today. So how did "they" know that I'd done it? How did "they" know to leave me the money unless I'm being watched *all the time*? But I did tell Silva I'd done the job. So maybe it is him after all. I jump when the front door slams. But it's only Sheeley, gone to see Grandad.

Ten minutes later, I'm getting dressed when I hear the door.

"Old GIT," screams Sheeley from the bottom of the stairs. I open my door, pulling on a sock.

"What's wrong?"

Sheeley pounds up the stairs, uncharacteristically ruffled. There's a red mark on her cheek.

"He threw the plate at me," she says. "He shouted, 'Get out, Geebo!'" I stand by awkwardly. All this is my fault. "It hit me in the face," she rages. "It hurts. He didn't recognize me."

"He just gets confused," I say. "You know what he's like."

Sheeley rubs her face and clears her throat. "You're right," she says and squares her shoulders. "We can't go on like this. He's gone senile."

"You'll have to talk to Dad," I say. "He likes you."

When I finally get downstairs, I'm Michael today – invisible Michael. Dad and Olly are busy in the garage and don't see me as I cross the back yard. There's the old Fokker, huge and useless. I climb in and pull the door closed. Behind the cockpit in the main cabin there's a sitting and cooking area. The sofa is still there. It's old and dusty but I don't mind that. I've got a little portable TV rigged up and I can get water from the tank on the roof. There's a big table where I can do schoolwork (as if) and a gas stove where I make toast and heat up beans. I walk through a doorway into what was once my parents' bedroom. It has a big mattress on the floor and an old chest of drawers. The tiny windows are so dusty you can't see out. A thin wooden partition divides this room from the back bedroom. That was where Sheeley and I used to sleep, but all that's left of our bedroom is an old armchair, some boxes of junk and a faded carpet. I run my fingers round the wall and

77

pull open an old locker. Inside is an old wine crate which still smells faintly of alcohol. I set it on the carpet. Inside is a red tin money box and a bundle of papers and greetings cards. I slot the fifty pounds into the box. I've got two hundred and seventy pounds now. It's my life savings.

I'm about to replace the box when a card catches my eye. I pull it out of the pile and look at it. It's a sixteenth birthday card with a picture of a fairy on the front.

Catherine
Happy birthday you crazy witch.
Your spells are too strong for me to resist. Love you
for ever,
Tom X

I replace the card in the bundle. I found it a few years ago in a box of junk. It's from my dad to my mum and is so unlike anything I can imagine him writing that I've kept it.

I wipe the condensation from the window. Over the hedge is a field that slopes steeply upwards. It glistens with dew. The quarry is sunk deep into the top of the hill and it is massive. It's roughly circular with a lake of deep water at the bottom. It's been disused for years and is now owned by the highways department. No one goes up there much. Kids used to go up in the summer to swim, but since they built the new leisure complex in town, no one bothers.

I pick up a cracked toy rubber snake lying on the floor. Grandad told us a massive water snake lived in the bottom of the quarry. He said if you even paddled in the shallows of the stone cold waters the snake would rear up out of the deep and snatch you away. He said it could sense your footsteps on the shore. For years I've had a recurring nightmare where I am paddling through lily pads in dark water, and suddenly a streak of brown and green, as thick as a tree trunk and as long as a bus, darts towards me. An instant later and the thing towers above, swaying from side to side, transformed into a gigantic cobra. It draws back its head and regards me, tongue flickering.

I always wake up as it plummets towards me, fangs bared, about to strike.

Of course there was the drowning. Every quarry has a drowning story to keep kids away, but this one was real. Grandad said one time a kid jumped off the highest ledge, known as Big Man, into the water (they still do this, sometimes . . . never me), but he never came up. Grandad said the water snake came right out of the water and grabbed him before he even hit the surface. Even now, when I'm old enough to know better, I don't swim in the quarry, even though it is only ten minutes' walk away from our place. The water is too black.

Grandad scared us silly with that story. But now I know it was just his way of protecting us. Now I'm scaring him back.

My pocket vibrates as my mobile pings. I've got another text message. I run my tongue over my bottom lip. What now?

FORD FARM GATE. 9PM TMRRW. WR OLD CLTHS, BRING GLVS + PLIERS. MORE ££ 4 U.

Here we go again.

Butterflies

It's late. Everyone is asleep. Me, I'm sitting up under the motorway bridge on a concrete platform, close to the top of the cut. I rest my chin on my knees as I watch the lights come and go. I'm hidden from the road. There's a big bush growing up around me. In summer it has long purple flowers that smell really strong. You get butterflies dancing round your head before they get sucked into the slipstream.

Everyone fights with their families. It's what they're for. Who can, hand on heart, swear that their home life is completely happy? Silva is the only person I know who doesn't have a bad thing to say about his parents or siblings, or maybe that's just Silva. He doesn't say anything bad about anyone.

A police car flies past. I'm not seen. Why would anyone sit under a motorway bridge at one in the morning on a cold March night?

The last evening Mum was at home, we were all eating pie and mash in front of the telly as she threw herself around finding things in a flurry of scarves and handbag and clicky heels and swishy coat. I should have guessed something was up, as Mum, uncharacteristically, was wearing lipstick and a necklace.

"Where are you going?" I asked. "The Ritz?"

She looked surprised. "It's the school reunion," she said. "I thought you knew." I remembered her mentioning it. It had been twenty years since she'd left school.

"Don't you want to go, Dad?" I asked, like an idiot. Mum raised an eyebrow at me. As if! Dad and Mum were in the same class. They'd known each other *for ever*.

"My idea of hell," said Dad huffily. "I don't think you should go, Catherine." He dumped his plate of half-eaten food on the carpet and Mum caught her breath. Then Dad left the room and thumped downstairs. There was a silence as we all watched the steam from Dad's pie gently curling into the air. A few minutes later and Mum had gone too, only she didn't come back.

That was it. One school reunion and she didn't come home. I waited up most of the night for her; then, in the morning, I got a phone call.

I'm leaving Thomas, Michael. You have to come with me. I'll come and pick you up in an hour. I got mad at that. Who did she think she was, ordering me around? And who did she think was going to look after Grandad? Needless to say, I wasn't there when she turned up to collect me.

I shift and stretch. I've been curled up here so long one leg has gone to sleep. I rub it to get the circulation back and watch as a convoy of circus lorries passes under the bridge. Maybe I should hitch a ride with them. When the lights have disappeared over the horizon I get up and climb the slope. I crawl through a gap in the fence and wade through dry, dead nettles to the field boundary. I cross the field in the darkness. I don't need a torch. I should know where to tread by now.

When I reach the yard I get a surprise. The kitchen light is on. I really don't want a showdown with Dad, and I'm too tired to deal with Grandad. I'm too cold to hang around so I decide to brazen it out. But when I get upstairs, I find only Sheeley, wrapped in her thick white dressing gown and sipping from a mug, her laptop open in front of her.

"Where's Dad?" I ask.

"Asleep in the office," says Sheeley. She switches off her laptop and closes the lid. Then she looks at me with her big, tired grey eyes.

"Where do you go?" she asks gently.

I stiffen. "Just out."

"Take care," she says. Then she comes over and for a second I think she's going to wallop me but instead she puts her arms around me. Her hair tickles my nose and I smell her shampoo.

"All right, Scrappy?" she whispers and I feel tears build up in my eyes, but I wipe them away.

"It's no good, blaming Mum," says Sheeley, stepping back and looking at me. "They weren't happy. Mum only stuck around because we were little. Now we're older, she doesn't have to. We don't need her." She grimaces. "Though I wish she wouldn't go on at me to move in with her, it's driving me nuts. I keep telling her I'll have my own place soon."

I flop on a chair. "We wouldn't both fit in that flat. She's deranged. She should have stayed here until she had something better sorted out."

"When you've got to go, you've got to go," says Sheeley. "They weren't friends, they weren't a team. You know what Dad's like; he's hard work. She's put up with him for too long if you ask me. They did NOTHING together, not even talk. I've counted the number of words they said to each other on an average day. It worked out at about one hundred each. That's not a relationship. That's a disaster."

I stare at my sister. She's got the same nose, the same chin, as Mum. "Have you really counted the number of words they said to each other?" I ask. She nods. I'm freaked out. What else does my sister notice? Does she count stuff about me too?

"You've got too much time on your hands," I mutter.

Sheeley examines her fingernails. "You're a boy. I don't expect you to notice much, beyond the length of your whatnot and what's for dinner." I scowl at her. Sheeley is usually above such insults. "Cool, it," she says, smiling, "I'm only joking. But they didn't even look like a couple."

That's true. Dad is tall and heavy, with dark long hair and a stomach which bulges out of his shirts. Sheeley says he looks like a pirate. But Mum just looks average. She's got brown wavy hair and is a normal woman height. She wears normal woman clothes, skirts and tops, with clean ladylike shoes. She likes soap operas, whereas Dad will leave the flat to avoid having to watch them. Mum likes getting up late, and Dad is up at six at the latest. They never go out; they don't read the same books (Dad doesn't read at all).

"They hadn't slept in the same bed for years," says Sheeley. "You know that. You've got to go and see Mum. This not-talking thing is killing her."

"Dad's an insomniac," I protest.

"Whatever." Sheeley narrows her eyes. "What's this Dad said about you getting funny messages?"

I find myself telling her all about them. It's easier than talking about Mum.

"Where are these cockroaches now?" she demands when I tell her I found two and transported them home in a matchbox. I tell her they were dead and that I'd put them in a skip. I don't tell her that one was missing, goodness knows how.

"Scrappy, not only are you THICK, you are also disgusting, and you could have been poisoned by the gases. How could you obey some mysterious text message? It could be from a paedophile or something. Are you insane? You've got to stop it right now."

"Oh, chill out," I mutter, wishing I'd never mentioned it. But I always seem to end up telling Sheeley stuff. Everyone does.

"I presume Mum doesn't know about this?" Sheeley twists her ring round and round her finger like she always does when she's worked up.

"Why should I tell her?" I reply.

"What are you mixed up in? Is this what you've been up to tonight?"

"No. I've just been for a walk. Look, I'm not worried. It's probably Silva. It's cool."

"You are being stalked and sent bizarre challenges," retorts my sister. "That's not cool. That's messed up. MESSED UP. Silva wouldn't do something like this."

I decide not to mention the latest text about the pliers, or the money I've already received. She's uptight enough already.

"You have to go to the police," she says. "I don't want to find you missing in the morning. Abducted by some old pervert."

"Sheeley, I'm nearly sixteen and I'm practically six feet tall. Who's going to abduct me?"

Sheeley looks me up and down and shrugs. "There is something in that." She looks marginally mollified. "I must stop thinking of you as my weensy brother."

"I'm two feet taller than you," I tell her. "I'm not in any danger. It's just someone having a laugh."

Sheeley shrugs again. "I've got a baaaaaaad feeling about this," she says. "A very bad feeling. Whoever is doing this has got it in for you."

"What makes you say that?" I ask nervously.

"They challenged you to go into a poisoned

86

building, like a lab rat. You could have been gassed to death."

"Sheeley, I'm a human, not an insect," I say, yawning. "And they use powder, not poison."

"Poison is poison," says Sheeley. "Next time you get a challenge, you let me know about it. Do you promise?"

"No," I say. And laugh at my sister's furious face.

"Then I'm telling Mum," she says, sounding about six years old.

"She's not here," I say. "So good luck."

The following afternoon, me and Grandad mess around with the plane. He's got his overalls and his work boots on and he looks like his old self. I'm feeling excited and nervous about tonight. I keep rereading my text. I've already nicked a pair of pliers from the toolbox. I feel a hard shape in my back pocket. This morning, when Dad was out, I borrowed his big penknife from the office. I want to be prepared for anything.

"They don't make planes like this any more," Grandad says, wobbling a little on his scaffold platform.

"No, Grandad," I reply. "It's over forty years old."

"So am I," said Grandad, "and I still work."

"Up to a point," I mumble.

Grandad taught me that these types of planes have a gas turbine which drives the propeller. In a working engine, air is drawn in and passed through the compressor, where it is compressed and mixed with fuel. This gets combusted and the resulting gases are used to work the turbine. Me and Grandad would get a massive kick out of getting the propeller going. I don't expect we'll ever do it, but it's fun tinkering around and it keeps Grandad happy.

Halfway through the afternoon Mum calls me up on my mobile but I don't answer. Let her stew. By the late afternoon, Grandad has grease and oil smeared all over his face and is growing tired, so I take him home. I look at the cracked pictures hanging in the hallway. What made me do that? All the same, I'm not owning up.

I find some baked beans in his kitchen and warm them up for him.

"I don't like these," he tells me. "I want a nice steak, with all the trimmings."

"What are you going to do this evening?" I ask.

"Telly," says Grandad. "I wish someone would take me out for a drive. I'm as bored as hell."

I shrug. "It won't be me, Grandad. I can't take my test for another year." I feed Jasper, who is prowling round, his evil yellow eyes blinking at me.

"He scares me," says Grandad, nodding at the cat. "He's always yowling at me and scratching my head."

"Then I'll kick him out," I say. And I grasp Jasper by his scruff, lean over the counter and drop him out of the window. "Sorted," I say, slamming the window shut. "Don't let him in again."

"I think he's a Geebo," says Grandad. I pretend I haven't heard him as I switch off the electric ring, take the saucepan off the heat and give Grandad a spoon to eat his beans.

"I'll see you tomorrow," I say. "Don't do anything stupid."

"Don't go," says Grandad.

Venus

Later, when Sheeley's in the shower, I sneak downstairs. It's eight-thirty and the freezing wind blows around my ears. It's still winter even though it's March. I can see the odd star. I remember Kennett talking about Venus so I peer up into the dark sky but I don't know what I'm looking for.

I feel the pliers in my jacket pocket. I can't think what I'll need them for. Twisting something, obviously, but what? Through the hedge I see the dull light coming from Grandad's window. Jasper's shadow is pawing at the glass. I have wondered if I should leave the flat and move in with Grandad, and look after him properly, but I know if I do that, everything will be down to me once and for all. I don't think I could handle that. He would wind me up too much. I haven't got a good track record with Grandad if I get annoyed. I do mean things to him. I can't stop myself. He still hasn't recovered from the time I told him I'd seen Grandma's ghost in bed next to him. His horrified face made me laugh and laugh.

But this is not the sort of person I want to be.

I pull my beanie straight, look at the time on my mobile. I've got twelve minutes to get to the farm gateway. I collect my bike and creep past the office. I see the back of Dad's head, bent over his desk. He scratches his neck and I hurry on, giving the Audi a wide berth. I creep past Petal but it's no good. She wakes up and starts barking. But as she's always barking no one will bother to come out and investigate. Then I'm out in the lanes, pedalling fast. I'm at the farm gate in just under ten minutes. I know the farmer, Bill Rogers, by sight. He owns the fields around us, including the one that slopes down to the motorway. Sometimes he comes into the yard after parts. He's a big hairy bloke with a ginger beard and a loud voice. Rogers is a few years older than Dad, they used to be at the same school, but they're not mates. Sometimes I see Rogers thundering down the lanes in his massive truck. He's got a sideline as a livestock haulier.

I park my bike on the side of the road and wait. I'm thinking I might go home and forget it, when my phone bleeps. I have to take off my gloves to read the message.

HEN HSES IN FLD. TKE 1 CHCKN. PT PLRS ON NCK. KILL.
LEAVE @ SID OF RD. REWRD = £60

At first I think I must have read it incorrectly. I reread the message, my stomach sinking fast. Kill a chicken? What kind of sickos am I dealing with here? I look out into the darkness of the field. This is nasty, nasty stuff, not Silva's style at all. Who is it? For some reason I think of my baby name, *Mr Mouse*. There's a grown-up Mr Mouse out there, creeping around, up to no good. I think of Judge. He IS pretty sick. But would he give me sixty quid? Would he part with that sort of money for a laugh? I've already had fifty; maybe I would get some more. Could I do it? Could I? I eat chickens, so it surely shouldn't be so difficult. But killing a living creature is savage. I've never killed anything bigger than a wasp. I get the heebie-jeebies just watching Dad lay out rat poison. I look around me, feeling the wind on my neck. But I have to admit, deep down, there is a small buried part of me which is wondering what it would be like to kill something. I decide to just go and look at the hen houses and see what I think. It wouldn't do any harm just to look, would it? Or am I being a psycho?

The field is dotted with little cabins. In the daytime the field is full of chickens wandering about. But at night they're shut away in their little houses, safe from foxes and other predators, though maybe not from me. I'm absolutely not going to go through with this. I'm not twisted. I'm not going to kill a living creature for a dare. I'm not. But I feel drunk, and like I'm on automatic pilot, like someone else is steering my body. I climb the gate and shine my torch at the nearest house. The plastic roof ripples and slaps in the wind and makes me jump. There's a wooden door fastened by a latch. That's all, no padlocks or chains or alarms or anything. Any nutcase could stroll by and murder or steal as many chickens as he wanted.

Everything in my life is locked down. The bottom door of our flat has two security chains, two locks and a top and bottom bolt. The yard is surrounded by a two-metre chain-link fence with barbed wire running along the top. We have the security lights, dog posters, a mad dog and two large gates which are padlocked from 8 p.m. till 6 a.m. We're not a very trusting family.

I find myself opening the latch and pulling back the door. I'm hit by a warm draught and a smell of shit and birds and sawdust washes over me. It's quiet and warm inside. I stoop and step into the shed. I can only just stand up. There are sleeping birds everywhere, on perches, on the floor, in the feeders, in the water trays – everywhere is a mass of white feathers.

Come on, I tell myself. These birds are all going to be slaughtered. What difference will it make if I kill one a little bit early? I don't know about chicken farming but I do know they don't live very long, and these birds look full grown. Without really thinking I grab the nearest bird. It is heavier than I expected, and it struggles dopily as I wrest it from its perch. I trap it under my arm so it can't move as I duck out of the shed. Outside, in the cold, it comes to and struggles as I fish the pliers out of my pocket. The bird feels very warm. It makes a gentle crooning noise and I can't help stroking its soft feathers. I never really liked the look of chickens, with their reptilian eyes and horrible red skin flaps. But this one is pretty chilled. I feel its pulse beneath my palm. It croons away, blissfully unaware that I am about to murder it.

I fasten the pliers round its neck.

All I have to do is squeeze the handles together. I shut my eyes and start counting to ten. When I get to about number seven I discover I'm gently stroking the chicken's back. I open my eyes. I can't do it. But sixty quid is a lot of money! And this thing will be dead soon anyway. It could easily be on my plate as a hot Sunday lunch.

I can't kill it. But I'm not quite able to put it back yet (it is now gently pecking at my sleeve in a friendly kind of way). I look up at the sky, hoping for inspiration, and see a bright star quite low on the horizon. I don't remember seeing one like this before. I'm no astronomer but I know my Plough from my Orion's Belt. It must be Venus! I hold the chicken up to my face and we look at each other. I can't commit murder with the Goddess of Love shining overhead. I'm still dithering when I spy something lying by the side of the hut. Tucking the bird under one arm, I pocket the pliers and get out my torch to investigate. It's a largish bundle, the size of a football, and is very still. Feathers fluff out in the wind. It's another chicken, only this one is already dead.

I'm saved!

I shove my living chicken back inside the shed and latch the door shut. I quickly look around. I can't see a thing so hopefully no one can see me either. I pick up the dead chicken. It's cold, stiff and damp, and feels horrible. Its claws are dirty and look disproportionately large. I get out my pliers and fasten them round the dead chicken's neck. I decide I need to do this for authenticity's sake. The pliers make a horrible clunking noise as I squeeze them together and I feel a bit wobbly. There's something mechanical about me as I put the pliers away, gather the dead bird together and start for the gate. But suddenly I notice a light playing in the grass just to my left. A pair of headlights are zooming very fast over the field, straight towards me. A third light shines from the roof of the vehicle. This doesn't look good. I'm trespassing in a farmer's field with pliers in my pocket and a dead bird in my hand. And who is it? Farmer Rogers or *him,* Mr Mouse himself?

I break into a run for the hedge, taking the nasty damp corpse with me. The gate is too far. I won't reach it in time. The vehicle is thundering over the field, the headlights sweeping over the grass. Heart thumping, I scramble up into the low branches and dead brambles and roll into a hollow in the middle of the hedge. I lie there panting as the vehicle passes by. I hear a cough over the rumble of the engine and I can't help looking. There's a man, not Rogers, hanging out of the window with a gun! I feel myself go cold. What is this? Are they hunting me? Do I make a run for it or do I stay put? The Land Rover stops a little way off and a powerful beam shines all over the hedge and down the field and back.

For a few seconds light penetrates the twigs and branches. If it were summer I'd be hidden by all the leaves; as it is, I hardly seem to have any cover at all. I lie still. The light wavers on my boot for a minute, then passes over. I hear men talking in low voices and the Land Rover drives off again, up the field, the lights sweeping this way and that. That's when I work out what they're doing. They're lamping. They're out hunting for foxes. The lights come down the field again, closer and closer; then they come back, illuminating the area just beyond my head. Then the whole world seems to explode and I hug my head in my arms and curl up in a ball, terrified. Are they shooting at me? The shot sounded like it came very close. I press myself into the bank, gritting my teeth, and wait for the next shot, wondering if I should try to slip away. But they won't expect a boy to be hiding in the hedge. They'll think I'm some kind of shootable vermin. Waves of hot and cold are travelling up my body and I smell gunshot. Should I shout out? But what if they're really after me? What if they are Mr Mouse?

Finally the Land Rover moves slowly on and drives towards the gate. I sit up. Now I can't remember what I did with my bike. Did I hide it at all? It could even be propped up against the gate. Just when I think things can't get worse, I hear a deep bark coming from the Land Rover. I hear the creak of a door opening and the thud of heavy paws on the ground.

"Go find, Meg."

That is definitely Farmer Rogers's voice. I shrink back into the hedge. No, do not go find, Meg. I've seen that dog before and she's a bloody great big Doberman. I don't wait for her to find me. I'm not going to lie here like some sacrificial chicken. Instead I slither as noiselessly as I can down the far side of the hedge. I crash into a taut length of barbed wire and scramble over, catching my trousers and dropping the chicken. From the other side of the fence, big Meg begins to bark furiously.

"Flush him out, Meg," roars Rogers. I fall to the ground, knocking the breath out of my body. I lie gasping for a few precious seconds and see the red eye of the reflector on my bike. It's lying arse up in the bank a little way from the gate. I hear something big charging up through the hedge and I force myself to my feet. I run the few paces to my bike, climb on and pedal like hell, shooting through the darkness. The air streams through my hair and I imagine I can hear dog claws clack-clacking on the road behind me but I whizz away. I fly round the corner so fast I think I might end up in the ditch, but I get my balance back and I'm pelting along the road again. A few more minutes, and I'm over the roundabout and the motorway bridge. I dare to switch on my lights, figuring I'm more likely to be slaughtered by a passing lorry than a chicken farmer on the warpath. I fly down our lane and up the track to our gate. I'm breathless, but also a tiny bit smug. Have I got away with this?

I decide to just check on Grandad and I find him

asleep on the sofa with the telly blaring out a pop star competition. I can't be bothered to wake him to get him into bed, so I just grab his duvet from his bed and lay it over him. I switch off the TV and turn off the electric fire. I find Jasper in the kitchen, licking up the plate of baked beans. I drop him out the window and slam it shut.

Now I feel calm.

At home, Sheeley and Dad are watching the same programme as Grandad.

"Where've you been?" asks Sheeley accusingly as I pull off my dirty shoes. "Is Grandad in bed?"

"He's asleep on the sofa."

Sheeley frowns and is about to say something when she is distracted by the telly. Votes have been counted. Winners are about to be announced. "But Talia's ugly," she mutters. "Ugly people never win this competition. You've got to have the whole package."

Dad shifts round to look at me. I see him clocking the scratches on my hands and face. "What's that on your hands?" he asks. "Is it blood?"

"What?" I look down and examine my fingers. Sure enough, here and there is a smear of blood. It must have come from the dead chicken after I double killed it. And there is a big deep scratch on my wrist where I must have caught it on the barbed wire.

"It's just a scratch," I say. Sheeley has decided that fresh, real-live blood is marginally more entertaining than the talent show and is looking at me suspiciously.

"How did you get it?" she asks. "Have you been playing with Petal?"

I open my mouth and start speaking and hope that the right words will come out. "I was looking for the insignia from the Riley," I say. "I thought it might have fallen in the hedge. I'm sure I saw it there once, half buried."

Sheeley raises her eyebrows. "Why look in the dark?" she asks.

"Because it was supposed to be a secret," I say in what I hope is a guilty sort of voice. "I wanted to sell it."

"Nobody pays anything for that sort of stuff these days," mutters Dad, still tuned in to the telly. "But you should have asked me first, Scrappy."

And the winner is . . . TALIA!

Sheeley screams as the onscreen crowd go wild. Dad swivels to look at me.

"I popped round Ted's cottage earlier; it's a bloody mess," he says accusingly.

"He won't let me in," says Sheeley. "And Scrappy has school. . ."

"Tidy it up tomorrow," Dad orders me.

I feel pressure building up in me. How dare he? It's his dad, not mine. "Why don't you do it?" I say quietly and Sheeley glares at me to shut up.

"Are you cheeking me?" asks Dad softly. I've got his full attention now. I look at his big fists. What good does it do to argue?

"I'll tidy it up," I say. I'll pay him back for this.

"Good," says Dad and turns back to the telly.

Sheeley breathes out.

In the bathroom I wash off the chicken blood. I look at myself in the mirror. I'm wild-eyed and my hair is everywhere. I try to read to while away the rest of the evening but I'm completely wired. I get a little rush of adrenaline when my mobile rings.

"What's up, Scraps?" It's Silva. I relax a little.

"Just hanging out," I say. I'm not going to tell him about the chicken. I want to wait and see what he says first.

"Bad news," says Silva. "We're back to school tomorrow. Every last roach is dead. We're free to continue our education. Anyway, Mum said come over for tea tomorrow, she's roasting a chicken." I remove the phone from my ear and look at it. "Hello, hello?" Silva's voice sounds tiny. "Are you still there?"

"I'll give it a miss," I say.

Night

Night-time again, my favourite time. My bedroom is full of shadows from the generator lamps outside. And if I stand and watch, I can make out tiny car headlights zooming over the top of the wall, reflected from the motorway, like a cartoon projected on to my house.

I can't stop thinking about the chicken. I'm worried I'm being naive about all this. Why am I playing along? I don't like the idea that someone out there is playing a game with me, even if it is only Silva. When I see him tomorrow I'm going to ask him to be straight with me. I've had enough mystery. In the yard, a small creature, probably a rat, scurries over the bonnet of the old Triumph Spitfire and into the open window of a Riley Elf. These cars have sat by the back hedge for as long as I can remember. Dad keeps them because he says they're antiques, relics from another era. They're not worth anything, though; they're too knackered. Their rusting hulks sit quietly disintegrating and their upholstery and carpets are infested with insects, mice and brambles. Me and Sheeley used to play in them when we were little. I was Clyde and Sheeley was Bonnie, speeding away from the scene of the crime: MEEE MAA MEE MAA MEE MAAA and BEEEEEP. We fought over the Spitfire because the black ball horn still worked. The Riley had red leather seats, which, although splitting at the seams and spilling crusty fluff, gave off a whiff of luxury. The slippery seats were perfect for taking mad corners, where you slip right off your seat and hang out of the car. Also the gear stick in the Triumph was as fluid and easy to manoeuvre as a spoon in jam. Now these cars have practically disappeared into the brambles. The bonnet has fallen off the Riley. The red leather seats are nothing but a mass of rusty wires, which would pierce your bum if you tried to sit on them. Anyway, I've got the old Escort to burn around in for real.

I look through the window into the office, where the lights are blazing. I can make out Dad's feet, resting on the arm of the sofa.

Downstairs, I creep out into the night. I am being Mr Mouse, I have made him mine again; I can move around and no one sees me. I have games to play with people who annoy me. I don't know what he looks like, because I have never seen him. But it doesn't matter because it is dark anyway. I am small and unseen. Shadows of derelict cars climb up the walls of the flat as I slink past. The generator buzzes like an angry wasp. The noise fills the night. The office door whines as I push it open.

Dad sleeps.

I gaze at him, his black and grey ponytail hanging like a dead thing over the sofa, his thick arms crossed over his head. He sleeps peacefully, an upset can of Coke seeping into a mess of slips and bills on the table.

Mouse-like, I sit in the corner of the room, gently shredding papers, bills, documents, even a cheque, watching Dad every second. If he stirs I'll be out of here.

"Now this is what I'd call cheeky," I say softly under my tongue. But now I've pictured him opening his eyes and seeing me. I'm freaked out by this image, so I creep back to the door, avoiding the crack which creaks when you step on it. But I haven't finished with him yet. I'm watching myself slide round the far side of the office to the lean-to shed. I pull open the corrugated iron door and step inside. The generator thrashes away on its metal stand. I lean over and switch it off. The lamps go out and silence floods the night.

"What's that?" Dad's voice belts out of the darkness. I hear little scraping noises, a crash. "Hello?" he calls out. He sounds confused, scared even. In the darkness, behind the office window, I smile and duck, as I think he may have glimpsed my outline from the corner of his vision.

"David?" he says in a crumbling voice. "David?"

Who's David? I can't think who he means. I slip back over the yard and up into the flat before he can rouse himself to action. Safely shut in my room, I look in the mirror at my dark self and wait. Eventually, an orange glow filters through the curtains as the generator chugs back into life.

I burrow into my duvet and put my hands over my ears.

I run my tongue over my sharp teeth and feel like laughing.

The List

Mum is layering cheese on pizza and half watching television at the same time. Her brown bob falls over her eyes. She's had this new haircut where it's long at the sides and very short at the back, so her neck is showing. It suits her, though no kid my age could get away with it. She's wearing her threadbare dressing gown, which she's had for about a hundred years. The colours have all faded to grey. She's got on fluffy green slippers and her hairy, quite fat, ankles stick out from them. I think she's put on weight since she's left home, but she looks less tired. She's wearing her nightclothes because as soon as we have eaten the pizza I am leaving and she is going to bed. She's just done a forty-eight-hour shift at the youth hostel. I've finally given in and come to her flat. Sheeley nagged me about a million times and now I'm here. But if I'm honest, the only reason I'm here is because I want to be out of Dad's way for a bit. He's in an awful mood; stamping and swearing and crashing around the office. I expect my doings last night have something to do with this.

There's nothing wrong with the flat itself. It's in

Gaunston, on the first floor of an old mill building, and it's quite big with high ceilings. From the window I can see the river raging down the valley. It has burst out over the supermarket car park and flooded the footpath. If the water gets much higher, the mill itself is in danger.

I switched on the TV as soon as I got here. Telly is good at filling in the gaps in conversation. And I'm not feeling very conversational.

"Well?" Mum says, sliding the pizza into the oven. She keeps flicking these nervous glances at me, like I'm about to smash the place up.

"Well what?"

"Aren't you going to ask me anything?"

I frown. "What?"

"*How's it going, Mum? Are you OK?*" Mum does a bad impression of my voice, making me sound like a caveman with a speech impediment.

She wants me to ask her about her. She's not interested in me.

"Dad's skint. Can I have some money?" I ask. Why won't she talk about Grandad, or her and Dad, or even, God forbid, her children? Ask me, I think. Ask me how the hell I'm coping. Tell me how you're going to make things better.

Mum looks away from me, tuning back in to the box. "Look at that," she says, pointing to the screen. It's the local news. The presenter is talking about a giant stag which is roaming round the West Country. Apparently it's the biggest wild animal on the whole island. It's three metres high from its hooves to the tips of its antlers.

"Ted was on about that stag," says Mum. "He says the floods have driven it out of its normal habitat and it's been seen in urban areas."

"I need at least a hundred pounds for food and for the phone bill," I say, staring ahead.

"All right," says Mum, suddenly looking exhausted.

When I was little I loved that ratty old dressing gown she's wearing. I loved how it smelled. I used to rub the cord over my nose, relishing the softness. I remember hanging out at the window, waiting for Mum to come home. Me and Sheeley would jump up and down and fall on her the second she walked in through the door. She couldn't get her shoes off because we'd be all over her. But look at her now. She's too fat and she looks old. She acts like she doesn't care about any of us. It's like she's suddenly past it. One minute she was the goddess; now she's just a grumpy old bag. If she even attempts to cuddle me I wince. It's like kissing your grandma on the lips; it's just not done.

To my alarm, Mum turns off the television.

"Michael. I'd like you to come and live here with me." She gives me a funny little smile. "I'm missing you, and I'm worried about you, stuck up there on your own. I know how busy your dad is. And he's not exactly. . ." She hesitates. "He's not very domestic. I'm worried about your meals."

"I'm not on my own," I say. "I've got Sheeley, Dad and Grandad."

"That's another thing." Mum frowns. "You aren't the right person to look after Ted. You should just be doing school and enjoying yourself."

"Seeing as how he's taken against Sheeley, and you've left," I say, "there isn't anyone left to do the job. I can't let him starve."

"It's Thomas's job, not yours," says Mum.

I'm getting really angry now. "You should be having this argument with Dad, not me," I say. "I'd like someone to thank me for looking after Grandad, not tell me off about it."

Mum looks a bit ashamed of herself. "I'm sorry," she says. "But I miss you. You should be with me."

"Come home and look after us, then," I interrupt.

Mum looks like she's going to cry and I shut my eyes. I listen as she scuttles off to the loo. Then I get up and open the oven door. I rip the pizza in half and drop it face down on the floor of the oven. Then I turn the switch up to the hottest temperature. Let's see how she likes having nothing for dinner.

I'm picking up my coat to leave when the door opens and Jez troops in. He's this gangly bloke with grey curly hair and a beaky nose. His Adam's apple is so huge it's like he's swallowed a ping-pong ball. He looks at me like I'm some kind of wild animal. Then he reprogrammes his face and shows me how he can turn on a smile.

"Scrappy, I didn't recognize you."

"Right."

Next door the toilet flushes and Mum comes back in.

"Michael, stay here, please," she says, clocking that I'm leaving. "We've got a sofa bed. Soon I'll sort us out a bigger place. You're not even sixteen yet. Ted's got enough to worry about."

"Bye," I mutter as I make for the door. I'll get the money another time. There's no way I'm coming to live here.

When I get home I make straight for the aeroplane. I climb the steps and let myself in. I sit on the stool in the cockpit. I smell oil and perished rubber.

I know Mum is better off with Jez, but I'm not better off without her. Any fool can see Jez would have a heart attack if I moved in with them. And I can't just abandon Grandad.

I feel under the seat and pull out a hardback book. *Aeronautics For Beginners*.

I open the book and start to fly.

School. I'm hanging out with Shane. Today I looked in the mirror and saw my dad's face looking back at me. Maybe it's because I need a haircut. Anyway, I'm taking this as a sign that I don't have to answer to anyone. I will make no effort at superfluous conversation. Today, God help me, I am a young Thomas Singer. I've even forced my hair into a stubby little ponytail to get into character. So here we are, freezing our buns off, trying to get some heat from the blowers outside the canteen. In our absence the river behind the school has burst its banks and the playing fields are flooded. The water sheets all the way up to the steps of the playground. Another metre and the whole school would be flooded. There's only three minutes to go before we're all incarcerated for the day. I haven't seen Silva yet. People are messing around, pretending to pick cockroaches out of each other's hair. There's nothing like a few unexpected days off school to cheer everyone up. And the floods just add to the air of anarchy. The only gloomy faces belong to members of the rugby team, too thick to realize their precious pitch will soon be buried in developer's rubble anyway.

Then Silva appears, puffing at my side, like he just materialized from nowhere. I suddenly feel stupid with my scraggy ponytail so I pull it out before Silva notices. He thrusts a bit of paper at me.

"Scrappy," he says, uncharacteristically worried-looking. "Look at this."

The paper has been torn from a notepad and is soft with use. It's been folded and refolded many times. Written on one side is a list of about fifteen names. I recognize them straight away. It's a list of people in my school. Even Silva's name is there, and all but one have been crossed out.

"Where did you find it?" I ask. At this stage I'm not worried. It's probably just a teacher's list.

"Alissa says it fell out of Judge's pocket," says Silva.

I try to think what this could mean, if anything.

"It's a hit list," says Silva quietly. "Every single person on that list has been got at one way or another." I read the names again; only mine hasn't been crossed out.

Scrappy Singer.

Silva stares at me. "You don't want those dickheads on to you," he says. He should know. Last year a rumour circulated that Silva had attacked a girl in the year below. It was all lies, of course, and we were pretty certain that Judge was behind it, but some of the girls avoided him for a bit. But when anyone mentioned it to Silva, he was so relaxed about it, even making jokes that he was too weedy to attack anyone, that it all blew over. After a few months the girl concerned admitted she'd made it all up. Someone said it was because Judge had told her to. Judge, of course, denied everything. How can you trace the source of a rumour? That's how clever he is. Silva didn't have a go at the girl; he was just as friendly as ever. I wish I was as cool as him.

I look at the names.

Shane Buckerell
Melissa Long
Frank Chevoney
Jack Scott
Perry Blackmore

I can clearly remember rumours going round about them too.

Melissa: will sleep with anyone for twenty-pounds (once she went around for a whole afternoon with a twenty-pound note stuck to her back, and no one told her).

Frank: murdered his cat by shoving it in the tumble drier and switching it to hot (he now has a cat graffitied on his locker in indelible ink).

Perry: has a fungal disorder in an embarrassing place (no one goes near him in the showers).

Jack: has got a secret wasting disease and will be dead by the age of thirty (no one likes to ask to check if this is true).

The list goes on and I can think of ugly rumours about all of them. All except me. It looks like soon it might be my turn. At break I sit with Shane and Silva on the wall outside the maths block. I am Thomas Singer. I like straight answers. I dislike games.

"Silva," I say. "Be honest with me."

"Sure," says Silva, waving at Melissa across the playground.

"Are you texting me dares?"

"What? She's lovely, isn't she?" Silva, admiring Melissa, is only half listening. "I've been invited back to hers for tea!"

"Cockroaches." I pause. "Chickens," I say carefully.

Silva looks at me, confused. "What?"

"Weird challenges," I say.

Silva frowns. "What's all this? I haven't been sending you anything."

I'm silent. I think he's telling the truth. This leads me to Judge. He's my next suspect. But I'm not ready to tell Silva all about it yet. I don't want him to think I'm going crazy. I didn't see anyone last night, only the farmer and his dog. But were Judge and Louis there, concealed in the hedge? Weren't they scared of the dog too? This bit doesn't make sense. There was no car, nothing. Had they cycled there?

"Scrappy," says Silva. "You're being a mystery man. What's the matter?"

"Look." I nod as two figures walk slowly towards us: Judge and Louis Saunders. Judge is well built, bigger than me. He's got black hair and deep blue eyes. He's good-looking and he knows it.

They come up close and I decide to attack first. "Hello, lads," I say brightly. (This is Thomas when he's talking to a good-looking female punter, maybe after a cheap radiator for her car.) "I hear I'm on the top of your hit list. I'm flattered you've finally got round to me."

Judge looks surprised. He's used to cowering from lesser mortals such as myself.

"We don't have a list," he says. "That's just propaganda."

"What's this, then?" I ask, showing him. "It's your handwriting and it fell out of your pocket." Judge twists it out of my hands, examines it. "It's nothing," he says.

"You're full of shit," I say, and Silva tenses beside me. Listen to me, if that wasn't throwing the first punch, I

113

don't know what was. Thank you, Thomas Singer.

Judge and I have some history.

Three years ago. We're all twelve years old. I've been sent out of my French class to run an errand for the teacher. I'm heading across the playground, behind the canteens, when I hear a noise like an animal whining. Then I step back as three hard-nut girls pelt out from behind the bins, screaming with laughter. They are big, heavy girls from year eleven. Everyone knows them; they make everyone's life hell. They push past me, making me spin round, and head off into a back door of the school.

I wait a few seconds and I hear it again, a muffled sob. I walk slowly in the direction of the noise. It's coming from the bins. These are screened from the playground by a woven wooden fence, made of withies or something like it. And when I step behind the screen I find Judge, stuffed into a bin, his trousers around his ankles and his hands tied behind his back.

I hesitate. At twelve Judge already has powers. Then I see a tear drip off his chin. Wordlessly I untie his hands (tied with packing tape which has cut his wrists) and help him out of the bin. He pulls up his trousers. I stand back, awaiting some acknowledgement.

"If you ever, ever tell anyone about this, I'll kill you," he says, his eye balls bulging with rage, like it was me who trussed him up and exposed him in all his puny glory. I walk away without a word. I know I am doomed. I did not humiliate him, but I witnessed his humiliation, at the hands of girls no less. From that moment I know I am a marked man.

But what Judge does want is unexpected.

"Can we come and look round your dad's yard?" says Judge. "I need car parts."

"Dad sells car parts," I say. "It's his living."

"You're his son," says Judge. "You must get them free."

I hate the way he's so arrogant; he thinks everyone will do what he asks, just like that.

"Forget it," I say. "You have to pay like everyone else." I'm not scared at all. Instead I feel exhilarated. I like being Thomas Singer; I'm invincible.

"Oh, come on, Scrappy, let us come round," says Judge, stepping closer.

"Or what?" I say brightly. "You'll beat me up?" (I can't believe I'm saying this.) To my amazement Judge sniffs and walks off.

"He's only trying to be friendly," says Louis. "It's nothing else."

"Yeah, right," I say. Louis looks hard at me. What comes out of his mouth next is a total shock.

"You know, we're not as bad as you think." He turns on his heel and walks away.

Shane looks after him in disbelief. "What does he mean? Those guys make life hell for everyone."

Silva shrugs. "Maybe they're lonely."

"I don't think so," I say. "They're a team. And why talk to me? I'm not cool."

"You're getting cooler," grins Silva. "But only because you hang out with me."

But this little exchange has me confused. Why didn't Judge mention the dares? He didn't even hint at them. But if he isn't Mr Mouse, then who is?

At home a manila envelope is waiting for me on the kitchen table. The postmark is local.

"College application form?" asks Sheeley, hovering. "There's nothing to eat for dinner, by the way."

I hesitate. When I'm with Sheeley, I find it hard to be anyone but myself. She has that effect on me. All the same, being Thomas has worked well for me today.

"It's nothing you need to worry about." I spirit the envelope away into my room. It crackles in my fingers in a promising way and sure enough, when I open it, there's a crisp fifty inside. I hold it up to the light. It looks real, but I don't think I've ever held a fifty-pound note before. I'm putting it back in the envelope when I find a slip of paper.

Congratulations. Next challenge. Kiss the girl you really want.
£75 reward. No cheating.

Whoa. This is the hardest challenge yet. I feel weak just thinking about it. The girl I really want, of course, is Frances, but she's way out of my league. I can't do it. I could kiss someone less lovely. But I can't shake the feeling that I'm being spied on and Mr Mouse will somehow know that I'm cheating. I reread the note. The handwriting is different to Judge's hit list. He'll have disguised it, of course.

The only time I kissed a girl was after the youth club disco when I was ten years old. One of Sheeley's friends gave me a big smacker on the lips after the music was finished. So now if anyone asks me about my sexual experiences (which is surprisingly often – unfortunately) I just smile and leave it at that. So understandably I'm nervous about kissing the hottest girl in the school. But I've got that familiar feeling, the little testosterone-fuelled lunatic inside me who says, "Go for it, boy!" Maybe I could kiss her. What have I got to lose? There's something about these challenges. Whoever is sending them knows exactly how to get under my skin. My real skin, that is, and not the ones I borrow from time to time.

Later, I'm eating a sandwich and Sheeley is doing housework. She's busying about, wiping tiles, dusting walls and generally being annoying.

"Sorry," she says, when a wet cloth lands on my head. "It was an accident."

I give her a hard look. She's wearing a baggy sky-blue dress that drags over the floor. She looks like a chubby princess from *The Lord of the Rings*.

"Mum says you went to see her," she says. "How was that?"

"She wants me to live there," I say.

"And?" Sheeley wipes down the counter.

"Never."

"I was afraid you were going to say that." Sheeley abandons her cloth. "What will you do when I move out?"

I shrug. "Stay here. Look after bloody Ted."

"You'd be practically living on your own," says Sheeley. "Dad. . ."

"Doesn't bug me. Unlike you," I snap. That was pure Dad; well done me.

Sheeley looks at me, long and hard. Then she says something which shakes me. "Where are you, Scrappy?" she asks softly. "Where has my brother gone?"

Frances

I wake to the racket of Sheeley's radio blaring out the usual early-morning nonsense. Through a gap in the curtains I can see blue sky. I blink and rub my eyes. I get out of bed. No, I'm not seeing things; the whole sky is blue and lasers of sunshine light up the yard.

I still can't get used to the fact that Mum's car isn't parked below my window. She's got a purple Fiat Punto with a Winnie the Pooh dangling from the rear-view mirror. I used to look out of my window at night and look at all the cars, lined up: Sheeley's mini, Mum's Punto and Dad's pickup.

I look away. I have a new challenge to think about. I switch on the shower and step under the hot water, rubbing Sheeley's pink soap all over me. After the shower I brush my teeth for ages and have a bit of a shave. Then I eye up Dad's aftershave. It's a neon blue liquid in a large rectangular bottle. For a minute I see it as some kind of magic potion, one which will make me irresistible to all females. But no one should put blue liquid on their face. I decide to give it a miss. I wipe away a clear patch in the bathroom mirror. I look OK.

I'm not one of these lads who spends ages doing his hair before school each morning. When my hair is wet and slicked back on my head I look a little bit like Sheeley. An idea occurs to me. My sister usually gets what she wants. Maybe it will work for me too.

"What are you doing in there? It stinks like a bloody brothel. . ." Dad hammers on the door. "Hurry up." I exit the bathroom, billowing clouds of scented steam.

"Morning, Dad," I say brightly. "Sleep well?"

Dad gives me a look but doesn't say anything. This is because today I am being Sheeley and I think he's a bit scared of her.

Downstairs I find a letter addressed to Grandad. Sometimes the postman can't be bothered to walk down to the cottage. It's official-looking so I open it (Sheeley would also do this and Grandad would only throw it away otherwise). The letter is from Social Services. They want to come and see Grandad next month to "assess his needs". I stare at the print and wonder what's behind it. Is this Mum's doing? What does this mean? Why aren't I delighted? At last someone else might take some responsibility for the old man. It's what me and Sheeley have been planning for ages. But now it's come to it, I just feel really scared, and a bit sad. If they took him away, what would I be left with?

Outside, sunbeams bounce off dented bonnets and shine in the puddles. The air feels crisp and fresh with only a hint of motorway fumes. I can't see a single cloud in the sky. It's Sheeley weather. This must be how

Noah felt after forty days and forty nights. The world is gleaming. Kennett said the best light for painting is after a rainstorm. I bet he's got his brushes out now.

At break I push all my other worries aside and ask Silva for tips on women. He's the one expert I know.

"You have to be brave," he says, settling himself on the wall in the playground and lobbing his orange peel into the floodwaters below. "I try to talk to them before asking them out so it's not cold calling. If they already think you're all right when you make your move then you've got a head start. And pay attention to personal grooming, but not too much. Women don't want to be knocked unconscious."

I'm glad I resisted the lure of Dad's aftershave.

Silva warms to his topic. "On no account should you try any stunts to get attention. You'll end up looking like a prat. Be calm, but don't worry if you go red. They'll think it's cute. And do not ask them out in front of their friends. It's just as embarrassing for them to say yes in front of their mates as it is for you to ask them. Do it somewhere quiet and you are most likely to get a positive response." He pauses for breath. I should be making notes. I'll never remember all this. I wonder if I could "accidentally" kiss her, like stumble into her and my mouth just happens to land on hers. Or I could just run over like a ninja and do it before she knows what's happening.

Silva is burbling on. "Most importantly, if you get a

knock back, don't be mean about it. Because now they know you like them, which is going to make *them* like *you*. So the second time you ask, maybe a fortnight later, you're more likely to get a good response. Once you've engineered a communication, don't break the lines. ALWAYS resist the urge to slag her off behind her back. It WILL backfire." Silva grins and slaps my back. "So who's the lucky lady? Anyone I know? Are you going to start by softening her up?"

"Afraid not," I say. "I'm going straight in for the kill."

"The lucky strike," says Silva thoughtfully. "It's high risk." He badgers me a little to tell him who it is but I'm keeping my mouth shut.

"You'll be fine," says Silva. "Melissa told me that quite a few girls think you're all right."

I can hardly believe this. What, me? "You're joking." I stare at my friend.

"No, man, apparently you're a bit quiet and moody but you turn female heads. There's interest."

Why didn't he tell me this before? I feel myself getting warm.

"You need to relax, man," smiles Silva. "Women are only human, like us." He looks at the flooded playing field spread out before us. "Reckon the water's going down?"

"Maybe it is," I say.

It's the end of the day before I see my chance. I'm on my way out of school when I see Frances coming over the tennis courts. She's on her own. Before I have time to talk myself out of it I find myself hurrying to catch her. I have a picture of Sheeley in my head. I am fearless and funny. I am lovable. I tap Frances's shoulder and my stomach is churning. She swings round and I accidentally bump into her. She looks at me and my mind goes blank. All I can think about is how pretty she is. She's quite tall and has dark brown eyes. A clip with a silver spider holds her hair out of her face. She raises her eyebrows and waits. I can't just kiss her, I *can't*. Where is Sheeley when I want her? I feel my lips moving and words coming out of my mouth. I have no idea what they are going to be.

"Do you want to go. . .?" I stop talking as a gaggle of girls arrive. Looby, Chloe and Daniella. I'm dead. No, worse, I'm Scrappy.

"Hiya, Franie!"

"Did you see the maths supply teacher? He is SOOO lush."

"Hellooo, Scrappy." (That was Chloe.) Oh Jesus. I can't do this.

"Do I want to what?" asks Frances, ignoring the girls who have now clustered round to watch. No no no! I'm breaking all of Silva's rules. I've not got to know her first. I stink of shaving foam and pink soap. AND I'm about to humiliate myself in front of her mates. Will I survive this? I don't think so. I just stand there, tongue tied, until Frances comes to my rescue.

"I was just having a private chat with Scrappy, do

you mind?" she says. I feel myself burning up. The girls splutter with laughter and drift off with their ears on stalks.

Frances looks thoughtful; then her face relaxes into a smile. "A load of us are going to the café tonight," she says. "Want to come? My brother's band is playing. They're pretty crap but it's quite entertaining."

"Yeah," I say. "Great."

"All right, I'll see you there. The band starts at eight." Frances smiles again and flies off to join her mates. And I stand in the middle of the playground feeling like a million-dollar man.

Now I'm cycling home feeling breathless and happy. Mr Mouse has done me a good turn. I would never have approached Frances without the bribe. I cycle home with the wind in my (clean) hair. I zoom in and out of traffic. I am going on a date with Frances! Me! She asked me! I can't believe it. Thank God for the Sheeley magic. I hope I see her in the mirror more often. At home I wheel my bike across the yard. Rain clouds are rolling across the valley. In less than an hour there'll be a downpour. Petal storms out to greet me, teeth bared. I'm in such a good mood I unscrew the dirty old milk churn just beyond the reach of her chain and fill a dipper of dog biscuits. I empty these into her bowl and back off as Petal piles into the food, crunching the biscuits with her lethal teeth. She catches me watching and gives me a low growl. I chuckle. She's got attitude, that dog. As I cross the yard it occurs to me that I should stop doing these freaky challenges. Maybe I should quit whilst I'm ahead. Hopefully whoever is bothering me will get bored and leave me alone.

There's a new wreck in the yard. My heart beats hard. It looks bad. It has a crumpled bonnet and a nasty smash in the passenger door. The windscreen is partially caved in. The number plate is YO22 WES. It feels like all the breath has been knocked from my body.

Sheeley's Mini.

Sheeley

This can't be happening. Car crashes happen to other people, strangers. Not my family. Not Sheeley. I force myself to walk up to the car. I run my hand over the passenger door. I can't bring myself to look inside. But I have to. I have to know what went on in there. No, I can't. If I saw blood I would die. I step back from the car.

"DAD," I bellow, "DAD." I feel sick. My head is whirring with worst-case scenarios. What if she's died? Is she in hospital? Where is she? I try to remember the last words I said to her. I think they were vaguely abusive. Where is Dad? Why didn't he leave me a note to explain about the car? He must have realized I'd freak out when I saw it. The pickup isn't here either. What do I do?

"Mikey." Grandad is in the doorway of our flat. He's wearing wellies and a shirt and underpants and holding a tub of margarine.

"Where is everyone?" he says. "I haven't had any breakfast or lunch." He clocks the car. "Is Sheeley back?" he says, brightening. "Could you tell her I'd like some eggs and ham?"

I find my mobile in my bag and phone Sheeley. She isn't answering.

"Dad!" I yell. "Where are you?"

Olly isn't here either. I'm trying to fight down the panic.

I try Mum's phone next, but it's switched off. Next I try Dad but it's the same story. What's going on?

"I can't find my shoes," remarks Grandad.

At last my phone vibrates and I snatch it up and answer it on the second ring.

It's Mum. "Scrappy, where are you?"

"No, where are you?"

"I'm running out of credit, and they don't let you make calls in the ward." In the *ward*. So she is in hospital.

"What's happened? Where's Sheeley?" My stomach hurts. I really think I might be sick.

"Michael, calm down. Sheeley's been in an accident but she's OK. She's OK, do you hear me?"

I sit on the step. She's OK. I clear my throat and try to pull myself together.

Mum then tells me Sheeley's in hospital. She's hurt her neck and back. She was involved in a shunt at the roundabout. She's got to have her spine X-rayed. Mum tells me to come and visit and then she rings off. I rest my head in my hands. For a minute or two back then I thought Sheeley was dead. I feel a tear escape and dribble down my cheek.

"What ARE you doing?" shouts Grandad in my ear. I ignore him.

The hospital is in Exeter, twenty-five kilometres up the road. How am I going to get there? I spy Dad's old Volvo, tucked in the garage. The keys are always hung up in the office. He hardly ever uses it. It is unlikely I'd get stopped by the police but it would be annoying if I was. Grandad's found a bag of crisps from somewhere and is munching away quite happily, swinging his bony white legs as he perches on the crane bucket.

"Come on, Grandad," I say, getting up. "Let's go to town."

Grandad manages the lane fairly smoothly. He's chuffed that I've asked him to drive. He's still got his licence so we're all legal. Dad stopped him driving after he drove the new truck into the river about five years ago. Grandad sat there for about three hours, the water rushing over the floor, before anyone found him. The car was a write-off and Dad went bananas.

Grandad's a bit shaky on the roundabout – I have to grab the steering wheel when he starts to turn the wrong way, but we only get beeped at once. I'm feeling pretty pumped up. Normally I'd be terrified in this situation, but I have to see Sheeley. Grandad drives a bit too fast for my liking, but he's surprisingly careful. He pulls out on to the motorway without any mishaps and soon we're tearing towards Exeter. Although I'm worried about Sheeley, I can't help noticing how Grandad does things. I remember now how he shifts in his seat, taps the steering wheel with his thumbs and blows out his cheeks when he accelerates.

We come up behind a lorry and Grandad makes to overtake.

Nervously, I put my hand on his arm.

"Let's just chug along in this lane, shall we?"

To my relief Grandad eases off the pedal and falls back.

I have to have all my wits about me when we get to the city. Grandad hasn't been here for a long time and the road layout has changed. I have to do the indicators, and sometimes change gear for him. But we arrive at the hospital car park without any incidents.

There's an old newspaper on the back seat, which I hand to Grandad together with a half-eaten packet of Polos. "Wait here," I say firmly as I remove the keys from the ignition. Then I head off to find Sheeley. Two minutes later, I come back. I don't trust him to stay put.

"Come on, Grandad," I say. "You'd better come with me, but no swearing."

We get lost straight away, wandering around the corridors, trying to follow the arrows. It's like another world in here. It smells of disinfectant and air freshener and there are so many people aimlessly walking about. We get some funny looks. Here's me in my school uniform with my tall old grandad, who's wearing a crumpled pair of overalls I found on the garage floor. But I forget all that when we finally find Sheeley. She's lying in bed on a ward and she's got her arm in a sling and her neck in a brace. I feel a rush of something in my chest so much I have to catch my breath.

"Been banger racing, Sheeley?" I say.

Sheeley looks very pale, but smiles when she sees me. Mum is sitting by her bed and stands to give me a hug but I flinch and she pulls away.

"Jesus, what did you bring him here for?" Sheeley mutters, looking at Grandad. I don't tell them how we got here. I just look at Sheeley. I don't know what to say but I'm so relieved she's OK. Then she turns her head and shows me a massive bruise down one side of her face.

"I got a bit of a wallop," she says. "I have to stay in for a bit." She explains how she was waiting to pull out on a roundabout when a big estate rammed into the back of her Mini. She's got whiplash and it hurts her to move her neck. The doctor says she has torn some muscles.

"But thank goodness it wasn't worse," I say, and bite my lip.

"Women drivers," mutters Grandad, so quietly only I hear. (And it makes me want to punch him.) We watch as he wanders off down the ward. With any luck a nurse will grab him and pop him into bed.

"Where's Dad?" I ask.

"He was here earlier," Mum says. "But hospitals aren't his sort of place."

"Jez was here, so Dad walked out," explains Sheeley. "I sent Jez packing as well. I'm not an exhibit."

Mum pretends she hasn't heard this and starts on

about insurance and how Sheeley will have to come back to hers after hospital. I can't really follow the conversation as I keep having to jump up and guide Grandad back. He's trying to strike up a chat with a woman in the next bed but she isn't too happy about it. To be honest I'm so pleased to see Sheeley I don't care. I hope she doesn't have to wear the neck brace for long. It makes her look broken.

"He's just as bad," says Mum, watching Ted. "I don't think he even recognized me."

I disagree. I think Grandad is a lot more clued up than he makes out. A nurse walks towards us. She's got the same brown shiny hair as Frances.

Frances!

I look at my watch. It's only seven o'clock. I've still got time to meet her, but I don't know if I want to any more. I'm too shaken up.

"You can leave," says Sheeley, watching me. "I've had enough of you lot anyway."

I grin. Sheeley sounds just like her old self.

"I'll give you a lift," Mum says brightly. "The buses are so unpredictable."

"We've got return tickets," I say.

"I don't think Ted should be travelling on public transport," begins Mum. But then the doctor comes over for a chat. I wink at Sheeley and drag Grandad towards the doors. Mum looks distractedly at me over the doctor's shoulder. I have to leave before she works out how we got here.

On the way home I'm feeling jangly and mildly euphoric. Sheeley's OK! She's going to be fine.

I don't even scream at Grandpa when he floors the accelerator on the motorway. Instead I suggest he sticks vaguely to the speed limit or I'll drive us home myself.

"I would love to drive at a hundred miles an hour again, just once more in my life," says Grandpa. "If you don't let me now, I never will. I might die tomorrow."

"You'll die sooner than that if you go any faster," I say.

"Zoom zoom," says Grandad.

"No, Ted," I say sternly, like I'm the old buffoon and he's the young trickster.

"I'm naughty," says Grandad, slowing up behind a juggernaut. "Your grandmother always said I was a demon behind the wheel."

I look over at his wrinkly old face, his gnarly thin-skinned hands on the wheel. Grandad hardly ever talks about my grandmother. Nor does Dad. I wish they would.

"What else did she say?" I probe, after a story.

"She said I was bound for hell and I'd drag her with me," chuckles Grandad. But soon after this, his face falls and he clams up, and we drive the rest of the way home in silence. He makes a bad mistake on the slip road, not pulling off until the last minute, and driving too fast. As the cars behind us honk like mad I swear at Grandad and order him to slow down. It's like part of his brain has gone back to sleep and I'm relieved when we make it back to our lane in one piece.

132

But now I'm terrified that Dad will be waiting for us. He'll give me hell if he sees Grandad behind the wheel, but when we pull into the yard, the pickup is still missing. Maybe he's gone fishing. Sometimes he'll take himself off for a whole day and just sit by the river. He's got patience, my old man, I'll give him that.

I extract Grandad from the car and bully him back to his cottage. I'm in a rush now. I've decided I am going to meet Frances and I need to have a shower and change before I go out. But inside the cottage Jasper has ripped open a pile of rubbish bags. Eggshells, tea bags and dirty old tissues are spread all over the kitchen floor. By the time I've got it all cleaned up and got Grandad settled in his PJs with a plate of pancakes and a mug of tea it's nearly nine o'clock.

"That was fun," says Grandad as I close the door.

Now all I have to do is kiss Frances.

Café

I get to town in twenty-four minutes, a record. But by the time I've locked my bike up and walked to the cafe it's ten to ten. My hands are sweaty and I feel slightly sick. I've had a crazy day. Am I really going to kiss Frances? She'll hate me for it. Kissing her without permission goes against all of Silva's rules.

The café is a normal greasy spoon in the daytime, with red-topped tables and a million posters advertising toddler groups and lawn-mowing services. Some days we come here after school. Now they've attempted to transform the place into a cool nightspot. The lights have been switched off and candles are burning. The tables have been pushed back to the walls and a low stage has been erected. The place is rammed. The band (one bloke on guitar, one on drums and a red-haired girl singer) are playing a rock song and the drummer is going for it. He's so loud I can only hear the odd miaow from the girl. Some people are shuffling round doing their self-conscious dancing. I don't see Frances anywhere. Then I sense someone looking at me. Judge is sitting on a table in the corner.

Perched next to him, swinging her legs and laughing, is Frances.

If I was Silva, I'd go right up to her and whisk her away. But I'm not. I don't have his gifts. My stomach curls as she clocks me. Now I have to go over. My feet move in her direction, but I have to weave and push through bodies and by the time I get there, sweating and clammy-handed, I've totally lost my nerve. Pretending to ignore Judge, I step up to Frances. She's wearing a green dress with black boots and looks amazing.

"Sorry," I grunt at her. "I'm a bit late." I want to explain about Sheeley and the crash. I want to say that I've been thinking about meeting her all day. I want to say that I'm gutted I wasn't here earlier. But I can't. Not in front of Judge.

"Don't worry about it." Frances looks bored. "It's no big deal." Her eyes slide away from me. I think I'm dismissed. I don't blame her. I'm shockingly late. Involuntarily I glance at Judge. He whispers something to Frances and she laughs. I'm just a spare part. I should get out of here. The drummer ups his tempo and the dancers cheer and I am swept away in a crowd of jostling, sweating bodies.

I linger in the doorway. What kind of boy am I? I haven't got the guts to just kiss a girl. How hard can it be? But I'm terrified. She'd probably punch me. I can't just leave, though. And after a while I see her again. Now she's dancing with Loobey. I remember what Silva said.

You turn female heads. There's interest.

But who do I need to be to do this?

Just then the singer announces the last song. I wait and wait and only as the drummer hits out the last beats I decide to be Judge again. I'm confident, good-looking and smooth. I have power. Frances probably secretly fancies me. I straighten up and compose my face. It's going to be all right. Now I'm back in the room, shouldering my way through the cheering crowd to her. Once again I'm on autopilot. There's a small voice in my head saying *This isn't the way it should be done*. But I take no notice. I'm Judge, after all; I ignore anything I don't like. Suddenly I'm standing right in front of Frances and I'm looking down at the top of her head. People are beginning to leave. The night is over. It's now or never. So before the Scrappy-me can talk the Judge-me out of it, I grasp her shoulders and swoop in, kissing her hard on the mouth, knocking her teeth with mine.

"Scrappy!" she mumbles, pushing me away. She looks so surprised, it's almost funny.

"Sorry," I say, as a giant blush travels down my entire body and I burn like a hot tomato. Where the hell is Judge when I need him? I stand there dumbly, not knowing what to do next. I want to run but my path is blocked by dancing bodies. Just then I am tapped on the shoulder.

"What are you doing?" It's Judge, the original model. His eyes are blazing.

"He's kissing me," says Frances. Judge's mouth is half open. He looks mad. As for me, I'm speechless. I run through my cast of favourites: Becky, Sheeley, Dad, even Grandad, but nobody is going to step into my head and help me out.

"Judge is my boyfriend," says Frances. "But even if he wasn't, you don't just jump on people."

"Sorry," I mutter. I turn and shove my way out on to the street, not looking behind me. Outside I keep walking until I suddenly stop and lean my head against a wall. I close my eyes and swear.

I totally blew it. I'm standing there, just breathing, when I hear footsteps in the alleyway which runs from the shops to the car park. Someone is running away from here. At first I don't think anything of it; then an impulse seizes me and I hurry over to the entrance. Just as I step into it I see a shadow slide away over the ground at the far end.

"Mr Mouse?" I whisper. But I don't follow. It's too dark.

When I finally get to bed I can't sleep. I replay the events of the evening over and over, cringing at my Neanderthal behaviour. I give myself cramp from curling my toes up in embarrassment. Now I know I will never, ever get Frances as my girlfriend. She and all her friends will think I'm a freak. But humiliation is the least of my worries. Now I've really got to watch out for Judge. I've just snogged his girlfriend! Suicide. . .

I'm finally nodding off when my mobile bleeps, and my heart does a quick skip when I see the notice "caller unknown".

Here we go again.

GOOD ATTEMPT £ ON ITS WAY. NU CHALLNGE LATER.

Why would Judge congratulate me for kissing his girlfriend? This means it can't be from him, but from someone who saw me this evening. Either someone in the café or someone watching from outside through the big glass windows.

"Who are you, Mr Mouse?" I whisper.

At school, being Scrappy, I'm avoiding people. I'm assuming everyone is looking at me and talking about last night. But Silva says nothing. He hasn't heard yet. Me, Shane and Silva are walking to class and I'm telling them about Sheeley's crash when I see Frances and a gaggle of her mates approaching.

"Quick, go left." I shove them through the common-room door. I don't think she saw us.

"What's going on?" asks Shane, but when I put my finger to my lips he shuts up. I wait until Frances has gone, then make to leave.

"Come on, Scrappy, out with it," orders Silva, putting out his hand to stop me. "What's with the disappearing act?"

I know Silva won't leave me alone until I tell him, so

I give them the whole sorry tale, everything apart from the text message which started the whole thing off.

"So you snogged Frances Hooper in front of Judge?" Silva says incredulously. "Are you insane?"

"Possibly," I say. It would explain a lot.

"You'll have a job bringing her round," says Silva. "Girls hate being jumped on."

"But I didn't really jump on her," I protest. "Anyway, it only lasted about a second."

Silva sighs. "You've got a lot to learn, Scrappy-Boy. You should have lured her away from Judge, at least. Chatted her up a bit. What's the rush? It's not good, not good at all." He frowns at me. "I'm not happy with you. You can't just snog women. You'll get a bad reputation."

"I'm not happy with me," I say. "But it was only a kiss."

"You crossed the line," says Silva.

Shane snorts. "Great," he says. "This just leaves me now. The only one who hasn't been kissed."

"It was just a mess," I protest.

But Shane isn't having it. "I didn't mind being useless with women, because Scrappy was too. Now I'm on my own. No girl will ever go out with me. I'm too ugly and weird." He's not fishing, he's just stating the truth. He is ugly and weird-looking and as far as I know, no girl has ever gone near him. Not one.

"We'll work on you later," says Silva. "Right now we have to cure Scrappy of these worrying psychopathic tendencies." He frowns at me. "There's only one way to sort this out."

"What's that?" I groan. "I'll do anything. Everyone thinks I'm some kind of stalker."

"Apologize," says Silva sternly. "And make it good."

After school, as I'm unlocking my bike, I get another message.

NW U'VE STRTD, NO GNG BCK. MTRWY SRVCS 4pm TDY.
£££ WAITING.

I look at it for a long time. Do I go? The challenges have all started going wrong. I don't want it to get any worse. If I go straight there after school, I won't have a chance to see Grandad. I bet he hasn't seen anyone all day, although Olly sometimes pops round with a sandwich. Mum rings as I'm cycling along.

"How's Sheeley?" I ask, without bothering to say hello.

"Asleep," says Mum. "She's back here with me. The thing is. . ." Mum pauses. "Jez has booked us a weekend away, and they won't refund. I don't want to let Jez down," she says. "He's been working so hard."

I just mutter something in response.

"Sheeley says I should go," says Mum. "What do you think?"

"It's up to you," I mutter. This is like history repeating itself. Mum used to try and keep Dad happy all the time; now she's doing the same with Jez.

"But do you think I'd be wrong to leave her here?

The fridge is full, and she's only sitting around resting. Jez has got loads of DVDs. She says I'd just annoy her by fussing round her all the time." Mum's desperate for me to let her off the hook.

"Why don't you bring her home?" I ask. "I'll look after her. What does she want anyway?"

There's a pause.

"She wants to stay here for a few days so her friends can visit more easily," says Mum. "But I did wonder if you'd like to come here and keep an eye on her whilst I'm away. I'd be happier if you were out of that place anyway. Thomas isn't looking after you. . ."

"I'll talk to you later." I beep her away before I say something really nasty. I always have to mop up after that woman. She's so selfish. She makes me want to punch something. I pedal on through the blustery evening.

Maybe I will go to the services and find out my next challenge after all.

Judge

Motorway services are ideal abduction places. Thousands of travellers pass through this place. That's a lot of fingerprints and a lot of number plates. Think of the clues that would be lost in the myriad of car treads; the footprints, the specks of skin and stray hairs, the grainy CCTV images of thousands of people. I turn off the roundabout and slog up the hill to the services. A couple of huge lorries sit silently in the car park, and there's the usual collection of cars; maybe fifty or so. Someone has attempted to brighten the place up with a tub of flowers by the entrance. Sometimes when the weather is too bad to hang out in town we come here. It's always open and they never turn us away, at least not in winter. How sad is that? Maybe that's why I'm jumping like a hungry puppy at these crazy challenges. It's time something exciting happened to me.

I hover in the café, drinking a Coke. Four p.m. comes and goes. I watch the car park for black vans. Isn't everyone who is abducted bundled into a black van? I wait on. These places are so weird, so transitory. I've been sitting near a family with two small children. I've been splattered with drops of yoghurt from the hyperactive toddler's spoon. I learn that the mum has swum across the channel and the dad is ambidextrous. The family have gone now but the leftovers of their food sit abandoned on the table: peas, ketchup and deep-fried fish in batter. Flakes of golden fat spot the floor and grease the seats. The little girl only ate half her apple; her tiny teethmarks are clearly visible. She'd coughed a bit when some of the apple had gone down the wrong way and the parents were beside themselves, slapping her on the back and laying her over the dad's knee. She was fine, of course. The whole episode can't have lasted more than fifteen seconds.

I got all this information in twenty minutes and now they are lost in a miasma of motorway madness and I'll never see them again. I'll go home. It's time to stop all this. Maybe I'll change my mobile number so Mr Mouse stops bugging me. But before I go I should get Grandad some chips for his dinner. He'll be starving, as I haven't seen him since yesterday.

But then my phone beeps.

IM HR.

My skin crawls. This is horrible. Why, why, why did I come? I stare round at the people in the café. I look at an old man slurping coffee and a young lardy woman burrowing into a cake. I eye a middle-aged man in a suit and shiny shoes gabbling into his phone. The woman serving behind the counter has very red cheeks and she's trying to make tea, serve chips and shout instructions through to the kitchen at the same time. So where is he? I twist in my chair, feeling panicky and scared. There's a bloke sitting in the cab of his lorry out in the car park. Maybe it's him. He's reading a newspaper – or is he really watching me? Who else is here? There's the gormless boy in the green uniform serving in the shop, the staff in the kitchen, a young couple sitting at the far table; there's people everywhere.

Just as I'm getting really freaked out, I get another message. I'm so quick on the draw that my fingers fumble the phone and it topples to the grimy floor.

FGHT JUDGE. HRE NOW. £100.

What? I read it again. Are they serious? This is getting sicker by the minute. I stuff my phone into my pocket and stand up so abruptly that my chair goes flying.

"Hey, watch it." A lad stands close to me. He's wearing a green-and-white-striped uniform and holding a mop. I stare at him, shocked.

"Hello, Scrappy," says Judge.

He's wearing a green services uniform with wet marks on the knees like he's been scrubbing a floor. Mr Mouse is Judge after all. I almost feel disappointed.

"The pay's crap, but the work isn't so bad," he drawls. He's smiling but I say nothing. He wants a fight.

"My dad's the new manager here," says Judge. "I can work when I need extra cash." He looks at me, weighing me up. I finger the mobile in my pocket and wait. I have no intention of landing the first punch. Judge flops down opposite me and deposits a dirty stinking cloth on the table.

"Frances is my girlfriend," he says. "So lay off her, right?" He grins. "I got there before you."

Why's he being so friendly? We both know we hate each other.

"Get back to work, Judd," screeches the woman behind the chip counter. Judge raises one finger in reply. The woman tuts loudly and bustles off into the kitchen and we hear her complaining about him in a loud voice.

"Silly cow," says Judge. "I wish Dad would sack her."

I happen to know that this woman is called Helena. She's married to Olly's brother. We don't bother each other.

"How did you get my number?" I ask, looking him in the eye.

"What?"

"My mobile number. Who gave it to you?"

"No one." Judge looks puzzled.

I'm silent. Is this the way he wants to play it? Is he going to deny the whole thing? I'm confused, though. Why would Judge be working in here if he had money to burn? Money to throw at me? I glance behind me, expecting his henchmen to appear at my back and demand all the money with interest and God knows what else.

"What's up with you?" asks Judge like he really doesn't know.

"I'm waiting for you to punch me," I reply, deadpan.

"What?" Judge frowns. "You're talking crap. You didn't know I was going out with Frances."

I look at him. Surely he's having me on. Is he going to make me spell it out? "This isn't about her. It's about your latest challenge."

I get out my mobile and hand it to him. Judge reads the screen, and for a minute his face changes and he looks like a small scared boy. Then the bluster returns and he looks like a sixteen-year-old militant again. He hands the phone back.

"Who sent it? Do they mean it?"

"You tell me." I feel myself getting hot. We stare at each other and I brace myself. I've never been in a fight before. Scrappy avoids all that macho stuff.

"You're not paid to sit around and chat, Judd," screeches Helena from the kitchens. "Get back to work or I'll get your pay docked."

"Oh get lost, you ugly cow," replies Judge. He may be acting friendly to me but he's still Judge, after all.

"That's gross misconduct." Helena appears at our table, red-faced.

"And you're gross," says Judge. "Go away, I'm on my

tea break." He's much more cocky than I can ever make him. Helena shoots me a look and waddles away, muttering evils under her breath.

"Who sent that message? Did you really think it was me?"

He sounds genuinely concerned, but I'm finding it hard to believe. I'm on his hit list, for goodness' sake. Louis is probably lurking somewhere, having thrown my bike over the motorway bridge. A car screeches out of the car park. I look over Judge out of the window but I can only see the taillights. Now it's gone. It was some kind of estate, I think. It was probably nothing.

"I don't know what's going on with you," Judge says as he stands. "But I've got nothing to do with it." He frowns. "Let me know when you find out who sent the text. I'd like to talk to them."

I watch him trail off, giving each table a cursory wipe and leaving a smear of grease on each one.

There doesn't seem to be any point in hanging around much longer. I get up to go and Judge gives me a really funny look as I pass, like he's unsure about me. Maybe he's waiting for me to punch him.

Outside, I check my bike for obvious evidence of tampering. The lights work, the wheels are fixed in and the tyres are firm. It's fine. You see how paranoid I am these days?

My phone beeps in my pocket and I jump like it has stung me.

I grope under my saddle and pull out a crumpled envelope. The flap is still wet from Mr Mouse's spit. He was *here*. Only seconds ago. I look out over the gloomy car park, a wet wind blowing into my face. Is he crouching in that hedge, or spying from the cab of that van? I open the envelope and inside I find a note and a photograph. I lean against the bike bars as my legs go all wobbly. The photograph is full of darkness and shadows but if you look carefully you can see a lad holding a chicken under his arm. In his other hand he grips a pair of pliers round the chicken's neck. The boy's head is half turned into a pool of light but the profile is unmistakable. It's me, Scrappy. All this was a set-up. I suddenly feel very small, standing alone in the car park. It's like a sniper has trained his sights on me and I don't know where to hide. I look beyond into the café window, trying to see Judge. Is he watching me now, killing himself laughing? I hold the note up to the light. The writing is scrawled, like it was written in a hurry. I don't recognize the style.

Another failure. New challenge. Get a souvenir from inside Newberry Show Home. At night. Reward for success: £150. Punishment for failure: this picture will be published on the internet.

I'm being persecuted! Why has this guy got it in for me? All this was OK when I was getting rewards for doing this stuff. But now I'm to be punished for *not* doing them. It's all out of my control now. If that photograph gets out, I'll be ruined. People will think I'm a mad psycho chicken killer. Imagine if Frances saw it!

Not only does Scrappy jump on women, he also murders poultry!

I'm tempted to charge into the café and confront Judge. Tell him to get off my case. But what if it's not him? And now the money is going up but so are the stakes.

About half a kilometre from the roundabout on the south side, over the dip of the hill before the road leads up to the wilds, there's a housing development. It's a mess of soil and rubble with piles of bricks and diggers and workmen-with-lollipop traffic control. But lately the cabins have been locked up and the diggers and JCBs have been collected and driven away on the back of big lorries. The single strip of green turf has gone soggy and is sinking into the mud. The developers' flag droops, torn and muddy and unreadable. Only two homes were finished; the show home and one other. Sheeley said that the developers ran out of money and had to stop work. There are deep foundations dug into the field, filling with water, but a little sales caravan remains on the green strip. During daylight hours, a woman in a black suit and high heels sits inside. Sometimes she overtakes me in her 4×4 when I'm pedalling home from school. She always roars past like she can't get away from the place quick enough. It must be hard trying to sell something which doesn't exist.

I'm supposed to be ignoring these challenges, but despite everything, I'm tempted by the money. Also I like the idea of walking through a house which belongs to nobody; a house with no history. I've seen the brochure (it came through our door). The show home bedroom has a fur counterpane and a pale yellow carpet. There's a shining white bathroom and a fitted kitchen with silver-painted cupboards. It's got everything. And now Mr Mouse is daring me to break in, like he knows that deep down, I'd love to live in a normal house, and not perched on top of a scrap heap.

But what if Mr Mouse really is a sicko? I'd be a prime target, with no one around to save me. I'd have to be crazy to do it on my own. I think about Silva but I don't know if he'd be up for it. I don't think he'd see the point. Anyway, he'll be busy. It's Kennett's birthday this weekend. Silva's family always have big celebratory dinners when it's someone's birthday. They light candles and wear their best clothes. Becky will cook at least three courses. It's a bit different from my family, where a birthday means a box of Roses still in the plastic bag from the services and a night with total power over the TV remote.

What about Shane? No, he'd be terrified and delighted at the same time. He'd do something stupid. The boy has no self control. He'd end up setting fire to the place. And afterwards he wouldn't be able to keep his mouth shut.

Someone taps my shoulder and I jerk round, but it's

only Judge. He's changed out of his green uniform and is back in his jeans and hoody. I quickly shove the chicken photograph in my pocket.

"Scrappy," he says. "I'm, how shall I put it? Disturbed by your message. I want to know who sent it."

"So do I," I reply. "And they've just sent me another one." I watch his face, trying to read it. But if he's behind it all he's not giving anything away.

"Let's see."

I guess if he's just sent this message it will do no harm for him to read it. I pass Judge the note.

"What photograph?" He frowns.

"Don't know," I lie.

"Scrappy?"

I say nothing.

"He must mean the new houses up on the hill." Judges eyes light up. "What is this, like some crazy dare or something? Is the person who sent the message going to be there?" Judge passes the phone back. "So when are we going?"

"We're not," I say.

"I swear I've got nothing to do with it," says Judge. "But I want to meet whoever wants you to punch me."

I'm totally confused. I want to believe him, but I can't. "You still haven't explained about the list," I say. Judge looks blank. "The one with my name on?" I remind him. "You might have set this whole thing up to get me."

"You're crazy," Judge says. "The list had nothing to

do with me. It's probably a teacher's list. Had you thought of that?"

"Don't lie. Own up," I say firmly. *Who am I now?* "Stop hounding me. Just STOP IT." I'm shouting now. I sound like Dad.

Judge frowns. "Stop what? You're talking in tongues."

He's right, of course. I'm talking in tongues and I don't know which is mine any more.

I'm lost.

Friday

When I get home the front door is wide open and all the lights are blazing.

I climb the stairs slowly, tentatively, not knowing what to expect. What am I going to find upstairs? The place is deadly quiet but the air feels loaded. Dad's pickup is missing so he can't be here. He mentioned earlier something about delivering some car parts up-country. I wasn't listening properly.

Upstairs I find Grandad reading an old newspaper at the kitchen counter. He's fully dressed, though he's wearing odd shoes. Overall he's made a good effort.

"Where is everyone?" he asks me.

"Gone," I say. The only thing in the cupboard is a tin of tomato soup, so I start heating it up for us.

I've really messed things up. In a moment of madness I told Judge he could come with me tomorrow night. Judge is big, like me. We'd be a good match for any weirdos and I'll find out once and for all if he's behind all this. I made him swear not to bring Louis. I don't want to get lynched. All the same, the doubts are starting to creep in. Why did I agree?

"Shall we go and sit in the plane?" says Grandad.

"Come on, then," I say. Someone may as well be happy. Grandad likes sitting in the plane at night.

A few minutes later and we're settled in the cockpit of the Fokker. We have a routine.

"Angels up," says Grandad. On cue I shine my torch down the dusty windscreen.

"Check for enemy aircraft," says Grandad, and we both look over our shoulders. Grandad always finds this bit hilarious and he chuckles and snorts to himself.

"My dad was a birdman, you know," says Grandad, when he's recovered.

"*Per noctum volamus*," I say dutifully. "Through the night we fly." This is all part of our script.

"He died in the Luftwaffe."

"Never in the field of human conflict was so much owed by so many to so few," I intone. We take off our imaginary hats.

"I can see the Bogie," shrieks Grandad.

"Release the pig!" We make a noise like an explosion as our imaginary bomb is dropped.

"ACK ACK," screams Grandad. "Enemy fire!" We sway left and right as we dodge anti-aircraft missiles. I lay my palm over the torch.

"Have we thrown a seven?" I whisper in the darkness. "Is it all over?"

"I don't know," whispers back Grandad theatrically. "What's that?" He gasps as I flick torchlight over the sides of the plane.

"St Elmo's fire," we shout together.

A few minutes pass in silence. Then Grandad speaks. "I can look after myself, you know, Michael. I get confused sometimes but you don't have to worry about me." His voice rings clearly through the darkness.

"Yes I do," I say.

"You'd be better off with your mother. This is no place for a kid. There's too much history."

I say nothing. Finally Grandad sighs. "I'd better get some sack hours."

"Prepare for landing," I say.

Later, Dad comes home and he's flying high, singing to himself and dancing on the spot. He's only gone and sold the Riley Elf to a clueless punter for a shockingly high price. Three hundred and fifty pounds for a pile of rusty metal! I hadn't noticed it was gone last night.

"That's business," Dad says, his dark eyes gleaming. He's even bought me and Grandad a pizza to celebrate. He goes off for a hot shower and I look at the congealing cheese and orangey tomato of my pizza. That car was an old friend. I thought it would be around for ever.

The next day is Friday and the sun is shining again. It makes the world seem like a different place. Like everything is going to be all right. Tomorrow is my birthday. I'm going to be sixteen at last. I go to the mirror to work my magic. I'm feeling upbeat. I'm going to be chirpy, helpful and charming today. Everyone will like me when I'm being Silva.

I make Dad a mug of strong black coffee, load it with sugar and take it down to him on my way to school. The office is a mess. There are empty takeaway cartons thrown in the corner and dirty plates and half-empty mugs of cold tea stacked up on the table. Pink bill slips litter the floor. The place smells of farts and BO and oil. Dad's on the phone. He ignores me when I put the coffee down next to him.

"The car was sold as seen," says Dad. He's irritated. Last night's good mood has flipped effortlessly into animosity.

I find a bin bag under the sink and start chucking stuff away: chocolate wrappers, old food, plastic cups, bits of dried mud off his boots, pieces of cling film, used envelopes, the lot.

"It was SOLD AS SEEN. You're not getting your money back." He tugs at his ponytail. He must be talking about the Elf.

"You wanted a PROJECT," screams Dad. "Stop WASTING my time." He slams down the phone.

I grab the bin bag and make for the door.

"I spoke to Sheeley earlier," Dad suddenly says in a normal voice. "She says the brace has come off."

I eye him warily. I know about Sheeley already. She keeps ringing me up with blow-by-blow accounts of her aches and pains.

"Does your mum want you to live with her?" he asks unexpectedly.

I nod and am still working out what to say when the phone rings. We both look at it. I can sense the tension building up in my father. It's the way he stiffens his shoulders and pulls and pulls at his ponytail.

"Got to go," I mumble and make a dash for it. I leave to go be nice and Silva-ish to Grandad and Petal instead.

School is a joke. We're watching an old BBC film of *Romeo and Juliet* but a group of suited-up developers are yabbering loudly outside our classroom about the imminent destruction and we can't hear the video. It's not exactly inspiring. Miss Hendy, my English teacher, isn't too bad. She tries to talk to me sometimes about stuff. She's asked about Mum moving out and said she was always here to talk. She knows I like reading and she recommends books. She also gives me amazing marks for my essays. But she only notices me when I'm right there, under her nose. I bet she doesn't give me a second thought after school. I look over at Frances, sitting in the corner with her mates, and grimace. I'm such an idiot.

Inexplicably, one of the developers starts repeatedly hitting the wall outside.

"That's it," mutters Miss Hendy. She storms out of the classroom. "I'm trying to teach in here," we hear her say. "Could you have your conversation somewhere else?"

"She who dares, wins," says Silva, referring to the school motto.

Qui audet adipiscitur.

I've been doing more than my fair share of daring and winning lately. They should make me head boy. I look out of the window at the flooded field and think of the countless football and rugby matches played out there. The freezing cross-country runs, the years and years of humiliation and victory as generations of kids busted their guts in the damp grass. This time next year, if they sort out the flood barriers, there will be houses lined up all over the field. I picture people inside, eating, working, sleeping and playing with their kids, like nothing else ever existed here. My eye is caught by a wink of light coming from the top of the shot tower. It must be the sun, bouncing off a window.

"Mum said to invite you to Kennett's meal," whispers Silva. "Want to come? She's cooking a goose."

I pause. I'm quite often invited to the birthdays at Silva's house. It's a laugh. We mess around and play games. Everyone gets a present. Not to mention Becky's amazing food. She makes banquets.

"I'm busy," I say regretfully. Am I? Do I have to do this latest dare? I think of the photograph of me and the chicken.

"She's expecting you," says Silva. "She's made your favourite pudding, apple tart, because it's your birthday tomorrow. Dad says we can have an Aries party!"

Someone has remembered!

"And Millie needs cheering up," goes on Silva sneakily. "She's just split up with her boyfriend."

"Sorry," I say as Miss Hendy gives us a meaningful stare and turns up the volume on *Romeo and Juliet*.

This show-home business is definitely the last challenge, no matter what threats I get.

At home time Judge taps me on the shoulder. I can see people watching expectantly as I turn to face him. Word has spread about the list and about me being on it. Everyone's waiting for the showdown.

"Are we still on for tonight?" he asks, putting his irritatingly good-looking face in front of mine. "My folks are away."

I want to go to Silva's.

"Not getting cold feet, are you?" says Judge. "Come on, it will be a laugh. Anyway I don't like mysteries. I want to know who's got it in for me."

I really don't want the photograph plastered over the internet. "I'm in," I say, but without conviction.

Silva raises an eyebrow when I join him in the bike shed. "You're getting rather chummy with Judge," he says, unlocking his ancient mountain bike. "What's it this time? Summit of the super powers?"

"He's not so bad," I say.

"He's unhinged," says Silva.

"What are you, jealous?"

"Oh yes, darling," sniffs Silva. "Anyway, I must go." He grins. "I'm taking Dad to the cinema before dinner."

Silva salutes me and cycles off, back to his big crazy family. I watch him, on the brink of calling him back and saying yes to the meal. When I'm with the Moxley family I can relax. The world seems like a fun place and I feel comfortable just being me. But I can't go. Not when I'm being blackmailed by Mr Mouse.

"See you later," says Judge, appearing from nowhere. He looks hard at me.

"Of course," I reply. Then I pedal off down the grey roads towards the motorway and my scrap heap of a home. The sky is clouding over again. I pedal fast to get home before the rain starts. But as I get closer to our lane a heavy feeling starts pressing down on me. It radiates from the top of my head and spreads to my arms and legs. I get heavier and slower, the closer I get. What am I going to find this time?

Look at me, I'm not being very Silva-like. I've realized something. I've been trying on all these personalities, trying on other people's skin, but it just doesn't last throughout the day. Things happen to me and I end up being Scrappy, like my behaviour is pre-programmed, like a moth spiralling into a candle. You can't just turn into someone else, no matter how much you want to.

Petal belts out of her van when she hears the gate opening, garrotting herself when she reaches the end of her chain, barking like a crazy wolf. When she sees it is only me she gives me a dirty look and slinks back into the van. I throw her the remains of my sandwiches.

Dad's out and Olly's on his way home, zipping himself into his coat and locking up the garage. I usually avoid him, but I'm feeling a bit lonely and he's the last sane person I'll see before I go out to the show home to my rendezvous with Judge. God help me.

I go over for a chat.

"You've heard about the stag?" he says. I have to think for a minute before I remember he's talking about the giant stag which is allegedly roaming these parts. "It was spotted on the bypass this morning," says Olly. "It's heading this way. Keep your eyes open." Then he climbs into his vehicle and starts her up.

"The antlers would be worth a fortune if it is as big as everyone is saying," he calls out of the window as he drives away.

I head into the dark, empty flat. My cereal bowl and spoon are still sitting on the kitchen table where I left them this morning, cornflakes welded to the sides. Mum would never allow that. I look at a pair of pink rubber gloves. I see Mum pulling them on, firing hot water into the sink. I see Mum's pink fingers close round the washing-up liquid and squirt some into the bowl. I see her flick soap bubbles at Sheeley, who is sitting at the counter, staring into her laptop.

Maybe this is what a ghost is; a space where somebody ought to be, but isn't.

I find a note from Dad.

Gone to see Toby with some parts, back sometime.

Toby is Dad's brother. He lives down in Helston. He's in the salvage business too, only he's got better machinery and his wife still lives with him. We don't see him very often. He's got two young kids, my cousins, and between them and his business, he's always busy. I kick off my shoes and turn on the television for a bit of company. But the picture is all fuzzy and the screen is jumping. Dad bought a booster set but the atmospherics are still a problem. I've spent my whole life with a jumping television. Maybe I'm jinxed. I switch it off. The buzz and hiss of crap reception is more lonely than the silence.

Last month, my whole family was slotted into these five small rooms, albeit in our separate worlds. Separate but together. Now we're scattered all over the place. I wonder if anyone is thinking about me, here on my own?

Sometimes I think the only person who is interested in me is Mr Mouse.

The phone rings just as I'm on my way out. I hesitate, wondering if Mr Mouse has got hold of my landline, but before I can talk myself out of it I grab the receiver and put it to my ear.

"Scrappy?" It's Mum, ringing from her hotel. She wants to know how I am, what I've been eating, whether I've fed Petal – stuff that she ought to be doing.

"Mum, I've got to go, I'm going out."

"Where?"

"Just out with a mate." Who would have thought that I would ever, ever describe Judge as "a mate"?

"I really hope you're OK," Mum says. She pauses. "I hope we can work something out. I don't think Ted's coping and I miss you so much."

I shut my eyes. I miss her too. I miss her so much it hurts.

"Bye, Mum," I say quietly.

Judge and I have arranged to meet at the services. I walk into the café ten minutes late.

"Who's this?" says Judge from a table by the door. He's dressed all in black and is drinking a Coke and fiddling with his mobile. A long thin tool bag sits on the floor beside him.

"My grandad," I answer. "Call him Ted. Don't worry, he's no trouble."

The Villa

Judge isn't happy. He takes me aside and in loud whispers informs me I've reneged on our arrangement. He says he should be allowed to bring a friend too.

"He's not my friend," I protest. "He's my grandad." I explain that Ted isn't like an ordinary adult. "I had to bring him," I tell Judge. "I have to keep an eye on him."

Judge watches as Grandad bashes away on the fruit machines and drops a coin, bending and creaking to retrieve it.

"Have you told Louis?" I demand.

Judge nods and I remind myself it's not too late for me to go home.

"I swear I've got nothing to do with your freaking messages," says Judge, reading my face. "Louis didn't want to come anyway." He pauses. "I know why I'm doing this. I want to find out who's got it in for me. But why are you going, Scrappy?"

Why indeed? Why have I done any of these challenges? There's the money, of course. And if I'm honest with myself, some of the challenges have been things I would have secretly liked to try anyway. This is my thing. My only thing. I'm not about to explain this to Judge, though. And I'm definitely not going to mention the chicken photograph.

"It seems like a laugh," I say.

Judge stares at me. "Are you sure *you* haven't got a load of people planted there, waiting to do me over?"

I nearly fall off my chair in surprise. Judge has got exactly the same worries as me. I didn't think he was scared of anything.

"I'm not like that," I say. "And who would I plant? Shane and Silva?" We both know these two are not fighting men.

Judge rolls the empty Coke can back and forth over the table. "You've got a thing for Frances," he says. "You think I've got you on a hit list. You think I'm stalking you and setting you dares."

"But I haven't planted anyone," I say. "I was wondering the same about you. You've got a bad reputation."

"People make up stuff about me," says Judge. "None of it is true. I'm just assertive."

I snort and his can falls to the floor and rolls under the table. We've cleared the air so we get down to business talking about how we're going to break in.

"It's definitely empty," Judge says. "I was scoping it out this morning. There's no cameras, no guard dogs, nothing. It will be easy. I've got the tools." He nods at the bag on the floor.

"Cool," I say, feeling anything but as I look out at the dark sky.

Out in the car park Judge goes to unlock his bike. "You won't need that," I tell him.

Five minutes later and we're driving through the wet night in the Volvo. Grandad's lanky frame is hunched over the wheel. I like the idea of a quick getaway and we're not going far enough for Dad to notice the missing petrol. Judge sits in the back. I think he's getting cold feet and he really doesn't know what to make of Grandad.

"What's up with him, is he senile?" he asks me, straight out, when we nearly go round the roundabout the wrong way.

"I don't know," I answer truthfully. "No one's got round to taking him to the doctor yet."

I think all of us are hoping this crazy, unpredictable behaviour of Grandad's will pass, and we'll get Happy Ted back.

"Where are we going?" asks Grandad.

"To look at a new house for Sheeley."

I direct Grandad up the road towards the Newberry estate. Then we turn off into the site. Dirty streams run either side of the road. We climb out into the rain, Judge slinging his bag over his shoulder. I immediately notice the noise. Like our place, there's a big generator buzzing away somewhere, powering the massive site lamps. We walk on a strip of tarmac past the darkened office. We see mountains of earth and bits of plastic netting and not much else. Anything of value has been removed from the site; everything except the two finished homes.

"Ghost town," says Judge, looking at foundation ditches full of water, the lines of orange plastic and the redundant piles of scalpings. The two houses stand next to each other. One has a big tarpaulin sign flapping in the rain.

NEWBERRY VILLA SHOW HOME. HURRY!
BOOK YOUR VIEWING TODAY!

"I don't think Sheeley would like it," remarks Grandad, rain dripping off his nose.

For the umpteenth time I ask myself why I'm doing this. Breaking into a house is a criminal act and I'm not a criminal. But now we've started, I can't seem to stop. We scoot up the garden path of the show home. The paving seems to sink a little under our feet and the turf looks bright green even in the gloom.

"It's astroturf," says Judge, wiping his shoes on it. We try the front door, but it's locked. Beyond the white rendered walls of Newberry Villa I'm looking at a brown muddy field, sloping up to the horizon, dotted with a few stunted trees. The sky is dark grey, and lights from the motorway glide over the field.

"Bleak, isn't it?" says Judge, testing the glass of a side window. He turns and grins at me. "This is mad," he says.

167

I really don't want to go in. It feels like a trap. I'm scared, but I don't want Judge to know it. Then Judge says something so surprising I almost forget where I am.

"It wasn't you, was it? It wasn't you sending messages to yourself."

"What?" I drop Grandad's arm and look over at Judge.

"You know, like a joke. You're not doing this just for a kick?"

"Only you could think of something as twisted as that," I say, fighting the urge to punch him. "Is this going to be all over the school next week?"

"Not from me," says Judge.

"Come on, let's get inside," I say. We walk round the house to the back garden, which is a small perfect rectangle of grass with a shed perched in the corner.

"Toy town," says Judge. "Where's the back door?"

But there isn't one, only a bit of board screwed on where the door should go. They haven't even bothered to finish the show home. There can't be anyone waiting for us inside if the door is screwed shut, can there?

"Michael, I'm cold," says Grandad. "Let's go home. There's no one to show us around."

I ignore him. The door is only lightly attached to the frame, like someone did it in a big hurry. My screwdriver is more than a match for the job, and without thinking too hard about what I'm doing, I remove ten screws from the panel. The door falls away before I've even finished and clashes to the floor. I hear the *ping ping* of lots of screws scattering on the concrete path. It means that somebody will guess we've been in here, as I'm not going to be able to put the door back properly.

Judge steps over the threshold. "Come on," he says. "What are we waiting for?"

"I'm not going in," says Grandad. "I'll wait out here. I don't like it."

"Grandad, you'll get soaked," I say firmly. "Come with me, it will be all right."

"The place is full of Geebos," says Grandad. "I'll stay where I am. You would too if you had any sense."

It's all going wrong already. No amount of bullying will make Grandad change his mind now he's got Geebos on the brain.

"All right," I say. "But wait here."

"Geebos," growls Grandad.

The Ring

*J*udge flicks a light switch but nothing happens.

"If they'd worked, everyone would know we were in here," I whisper in annoyance. I feel my way along the wall. We're in a lobby with three doors leading off. "Don't touch anything else until we've searched the place." I look round. "Judge?"

He's not there. A worm of worry squirms in my guts. Is this where it all starts? Are there others waiting for me in the next room? The house is deadly quiet. I've just made up my mind to walk straight back out the door and go home when Judge pops his head round the far door and I nearly scream out loud.

"It's a bloody dump," he says. He steps out and walks bang into the wall. "Ouch," he says humorously.

I breathe out. Tell myself to chill. I step into a kitchen with immaculate surfaces and a tiled floor. On the counter there's a bowl full of wrinkled lemons. We go through an arch into a living room. There's a deep carpet, a white sofa and a shelf full of books. A coffee table is set with two glasses full of plastic ice. Judge takes a book out and I cringe as he lobs it at me, but it glances off my arm and falls to the floor. It's a hollow book. The whole place is a sham. It isn't so interesting to be in here now we've broken in. It's just a sad faked-up house.

I go back into the lobby and run up the stairs. I have to make sure there's no one else here.

"Hey, wait up." Judge pounds up the stairs after me. If Mr Mouse is lurking (and I don't see how he could have got in and screwed up the door behind him) he'll have been well and truly alerted to our presence. But all we find upstairs is a small white bathroom and three immaculate bedrooms. We step into the master bedroom. Light pours in through the windows from the big lamp outside, giving the room an orangey glow. There's a huge double bed, complete with a furry counterpane and matching cushions.

It's like a theatre set.

I step over to the window and see the motorway down in the valley with its rows of twinkling lights. Judge stands next to me, staring out into the darkness through his binoculars. What is the point of that? As we look I hear a car engine start up, and a pair of headlights slowly reverses out of the complex.

"Grandad!" I bellow. I know it's him because one of the Volvo headlamps is dimmer than the other. I should have taken the keys with me.

"We'll never catch him," says Judge, putting the binoculars down. "Let's go."

"I thought you wanted to stay and meet Mr Mouse," I say slowly. "Wasn't that the idea?"

"Who's Mr Mouse?" replies Judge, looking at me strangely.

I'm about to reply when my mobile beeps. I've got a message. I look at Judge. He can't have sent it because I can see his hands cupped round his binoculars.

"Go on," he whispers. "What does it say?"

I pull my phone out of my pocket. It's tricky because my hands are trembling. I push the button and the text comes up.

IF U WNT 2 C UR SISTR AGN, GO 2 QURRY @ 7 AM

A pressure builds up in my head. This can't be real. This isn't happening. I back against the wall. I can't think.

"What does it say?" asks Judge.

I nearly drop the phone as I pass it to him.

"That's sick," says Judge, reading it. "But Scrappy, it's just someone having a laugh."

I have my hand over my mouth. I think it is to stop me from screaming.

Sheeley!

Judge is passing the phone back when it vibrates in my hand and I let go and it falls to the floor, beeping. It's another message. I pick up the phone cautiously, like it might burn me, and read.

NT JKING. C MSTR BDRM WNDW.

I shine the torch on the window but can't see anything on the glass, no message or anything. But something is glinting on the window ledge. I walk over the soft, deep carpet and pick up a small shiny object. I gasp and feel my knees buckle.

It's Sheeley's ring. I reach out and pick it up carefully, as if it's going to sting me.

Judge takes my mobile from me, reads the screen and swears. I stumble backwards and fall on the bed and retch and retch. My mind is racing with all sorts of hideous images.

"Listen," shouts Judge, and as I force myself to my feet, sick with terror, I can hear *another* car reverse out of the car park. The driver has not turned on his headlights.

It's Mr Mouse. I know it.

"Get out!" I yell, and we turn and pound down the stairs and out of the door like our arses are on fire.

"What about the door?" calls Judge as we fall out into the garden.

"Forget it," I grunt. We crash down the path and back out to the building site. I'm holding Sheeley's ring so tightly it cuts into my palm. But we're way too late to catch up with the second car. We skid into the empty car park.

Whoever it was has gone.

"Come on," calls Judge. He's hurrying out of the estate to the road, his bag bouncing off his shoulder. He's had enough of this place and so have I. But as I run to catch him up I get my phone out of my pocket and dial Sheeley's number. The cold air burns my lungs. As I run I listen for the clicks and the dial tone but instead I hear a posh woman's voice.

Sorry, the person you are calling is unable to take your call. Please try again later.

I try again, but I get the same. I stuff the phone in my pocket and sprint after Judge down the dark road, away from that place. It's quiet; the few cars that pass seem to take no notice of us: two lads, running through the dark. I want to flag them down and scream for help.

My sister is in danger. I don't know what to do.

We reach the services in about ten minutes and stand panting in the porch. I have to bend over, put my hands on my knees. When I straighten up Judge is watching me with wide, wide eyes. I don't think he's Mr Mouse any more.

"Scrappy, are you winding me up?" Almost as soon as he's said it I get a beeping from my phone. Maybe it's Sheeley; I read the message.

2 KP HER SAFE DO NT TELL ANYNE, NT FMLY, NT POLCE.
I'M WTCHNG

"What does it say?" asks Judge.

"I've got to go," I croak. "I need to make sure Ted's gone home."

Judge breathes out. Abruptly he walks off, pushing through the heavy doors into the steamy chip-smelling services. The doors swing shut with a squeak. I look through the lighted window of the café. The place is pretty empty; there's only a young couple arguing at the other end of the room and a tired-looking old man sipping a coffee.

I want to phone Mum, Dad, anyone. But I'm too scared. I've got to keep Sheeley safe. I want to cry. I've got to walk home now, through the dark lanes and God knows what else. I've got to cross the empty yard and hope to hell Mr Mouse isn't lying in wait for me. I feel sick and cold. I feel like I'm falling, with no one to catch me. I'm alone. But I've got to keep going. I'll walk up through the fields. That way, I'll feel safer. I'm used to the fields at night.

"Come on." A voice next to me almost makes me shout out in alarm. But it's just Judge. He's perched on his bike, his face grim. "I'll give you a backy."

Big Man

The motorway is quiet under the bridge. Only one set of lights cruise through the darkness. I hope to hell Grandad isn't out there. I should never have left him. I'm balancing on Judge's narrow saddle, legs held out like the metal is burning, and leaning away from Judge's arse as he pedals us through the darkness. I can see from here that the generator has failed yet again. Usually there's a brown glow coming over the hedge from the main yard lamp. Now it's all darkness.

"Why are you helping me?" I ask Judge as we spin through the deep lane.

"Christ, Scrappy. I'm not as bad as everyone makes out. How could I let you face this on your own?"

This is something I will think about some other time; the possibility that Judge has a human side. We crunch off the road up to the yard and I dismount.

For once Petal's barking doesn't make me angry. It's good to hear something normal in this terrifying night.

"Hey, girl," I whisper as we pass through the gate. I

go up to her and slip off her chain. If Mr Mouse is waiting for me then I need all the help I can get. But Petal, the traitor, bounds off into the darkness.

"I can't see a thing," Judge says unnecessarily (can Mr Mouse hear him?) and he flips off his bike lights and hands me one.

It's blowy and starting to rain and I'm tingling. I know, just know, that Mr Mouse is watching me. The fear is awful. I'm listening, looking, trying to sense where he is. Is he holed up in the office? Behind that stack of cars? Is he lurking in the garage, or has he crept into the flat, and is now watching us from my own bedroom window?

Where is he?

"Where's your family?" whispers Judge. Where indeed? I don't reply. I look from left to right, weave through the cars and round the office.

Dad's pickup is still missing.

"Look." Judge points in the gloom and there, next to the plane, is the Volvo, and the front door is hanging open. I race over and check it. Empty. But at least Grandad isn't motoring around any more. I reach in and remove the keys from the ignition. Then I climb the stairs into the plane, Judge following close behind.

"This is so cool," Judge can't help spluttering. "It's huge." And for a minute I forget everything else and just think about how Judge, Judge!, is here, in my plane, in my place, and I don't mind.

"Ted?" I call into the cabin and shine my torch round. There's Grandad, so asleep he looks dead, stretched out on the sofa, his head hanging back. He breathes out a soft snore. Relieved, I creep over and cover him with a blanket. He's safe. Now I can focus on Sheeley.

Judge follows me out of the plane, though I can tell he's dying to poke around. I search around the undercarriage. Judge watches as I dive into the boot of the Volvo and pull out what I'm searching for.

A tow rope.

"What are you going to do with that?" whispers Judge.

"Don't you want to go home?" I ask him. "You don't want to hang around here."

Judge shrugs. He's soaked and his teeth are chattering. "I can't leave you on your own," he says. "Not with all this going on."

"I'm touched," I say brusquely. Though really I don't want him to go either. I don't want to be left here in the dark with my mad old grandad and Mr Mouse.

"Petal?" I call hoarsely. "Petal?" I feel something brush against my legs and I step back to see Petal's eyes glinting up at me.

"Good girl," I say. "Good dog." I tie her to the aeroplane steps.

I'm not going in the flat. I don't think my feet would go up the stairs. I can't stop thinking that Mr Mouse is hiding somewhere inside. (And where is he keeping Sheeley?)

I tell Judge we'll spend the night in the plane with Grandad.

"I still think you should call the police if you're really worried," says Judge.

"It's not your sister," I reply.

Inside the plane I pull the door hard and tie the handle shut, my fingers fumbling from the wet and cold. Judge looks a bit worried as I do this, but says nothing. And me, I'm feeling a bit safer.

No one gets past Petal.

It's late, so late. It's the dead of night. I wipe the misty window but it doesn't help. I can't see much. Outside, Petal is curled up under the steps, sleeping. Everyone is sleeping. Grandad on his sofa, and eventually, Judge too. He'd called up Louis in front of my nose and told him where he was.

"Just in case," he said to me afterwards.

In case of what? Now he's sleeping on the floor under some old coats.

Me, I'm awake. Wide awake. I'm trying Sheeley's mobile over and over. I'm on the point of calling the police a million times. I gaze out of the dark, rain-dribbled window until eventually my reflection twists into all kinds of grotesque shapes. I keep picturing Sheeley, shut into some dark room, crying. But really I'm finding it hard to believe this is happening.

Outside it's getting light. The sky is a dark blue and the roar from the motorway is growing louder. I ought to be exhausted after the night I've had, but I'm not; I'm fizzing with adrenaline. I try Sheeley's phone once again, just in case, but it's no use. She's not answering. I think of Sheeley standing on her head at her ninth birthday party. Everyone was clapping and cheering her on. She must have stayed up for at least five minutes before she passed out and toppled over. Being Sheeley she was back in the thick of the party in about two minutes. Sheeley doesn't like to miss out on anything.

It's half past six. In the blue light Judge and Grandad look like aliens. Leaving them sleeping, I untie the string and creep out the door.

Here we go.

I walk steadily uphill towards the quarry, my calf muscles burning and my lungs aching. I don't want to think about whether I'm doing the right thing. It's too late for that.

I can't block out my fear. I'm really scared. I'm scared for Sheeley and for me. What's Mr Mouse going to make me do next? Is he going to be up here? Is he going to set me another challenge or something worse? I tell myself I'm a big lad. I'm a match for an adult. But I should have brought some kind of weapon; even a stick would be better than nothing. But who am I trying to fool? I don't want to fight anyone. I just want all this to end. For the millionth time I wish I'd never played along with the dares.

Scrappy is an idiot.

As I climb a mist floats down to meet me. The temperature is dropping. As I reach the top I hear a rustle in the hedge. It's the sound of someone walking on dead leaves and snapping twigs. I stop, ready to turn and belt off. I hold my breath as the noise gets closer. Whatever it is walks on the other side of the hedge, getting nearer and nearer. Now I can hear two people's footsteps. This is it.

I'm frozen, staring in the direction of the noise. Then it stops and the whole world seems to go still and silent.

"Sheeley?"

I fall back as something massive bursts through the hedge and skitters into the field. I take a few paces back as an enormous creature stands staring at me through big dark eyes. It's a stag. The stag. His antlers are huge, heavy things, like weapons. Steam rises from his neck and pours out of his velvety nostrils. He towers over me, smelling of hot earth and wet hair. We look at each other and I don't dare move a muscle. I swear he's looking deep into my eyes. I can't breathe, wondering if he's going to attack. I can't believe a thing like this is loose and roaming around. I didn't know deer could get this big. He's like a creature from another age. I think of all the newspaper reports about him. For a second I feel a kinship with him. I, too, know what it is like to be hunted.

"Hello," I whisper.

He snorts and in an instant he's bounded down the

field and is gone. A few muddy prints is all that is left of him.

A few minutes pass before I'm together enough to move. I'm just looking at a misty field, and below that, our yard with the wrecks piled high – and beyond that, the motorway.

The cars are backed up on the northbound side as far as I can see. It's another world down there. I check the time. It's five to seven. I haven't got time to wait. I push through a gap in the hedge and now I'm in a large, exposed area at the top of the hill. There are no cars, no footprints and no sounds (except, as ever, the grumbling motorway). Tall padlocked gates stand ahead of me. I make for the hole in the fence that's been there for years. I squeeze through and walk out into the open. A wide shale trackway spirals down to the edge of the quarry, finally disappearing into the black water below. There are signs dotted around everywhere.

DANGER – KEEP AWAY

PRIVATE PROPERTY

DANGER – LOOSE STONES

DANGER – DEEP WATER

There's no one up here except me. Or at least, no one I can see. Mr Mouse could be spying on me from the far hill, or from behind the hedge, or behind any of the boulders that litter the quarry slopes. He's everywhere and nowhere, like a bloody ghost.

I stand at the edge of the quarry behind the battered barbed-wire fence which sticks out of the dead grass at the edge of the cliff. I reassure myself that if someone came up behind me and pushed, I'd only slither down the slate and shale to the trackway, some three metres below. But there's a sheer drop if I walk a little further. There are wide ledges at intervals, going down the face. The highest is close to me, just jutting out from the trackway. If you jumped there, you'd fall like a stone directly into the water. This is Big Man, the highest ledge, the place where the kid jumped, the one who never came back. I look down into the lake in the bottom of the pit. It is absolutely black and still.

It's my birthday. I'm sixteen at last. I never dreamed it would be like this. I thought when I turned sixteen, everything would change, that life would somehow get better. Now look at me!

I wait on the top of the cliff, nervous, coiled. At last my mobile beeps and a sharp chill rushes the length of my body. I have to hold my nerve.

Here he is.

IF U WNT 2 C UR SSTR AGN U HV 2 JMP FRM BIG MAN

I feel my mouth fall open and the cold rushes come again and again. How can he be serious? I can't jump. It would be suicide. I'd be dead of fear before I even hit the water. I read it again. Of course it is serious. It's been serious all along. This is what everything has been leading up to, from the cockroaches to the chicken to the date, everything. And I'm not being offered money any more. It's gone too far for that. Now I'm doing it for my sister. Someone out there must really hate us. I walk over to Big Man and look over the edge. It's a long way down. I step back. I can't do it. I force myself to look over again. There's no reflection in the dark water. It's opaque and dense. God knows what's under there. I don't believe in the water snake, of course. But all those years of nightmares have ingrained a terror of this place into me. It's an illogical fear, but it is there. In my mind's eye I see the massive eel coiling slowly under the surface, waiting, listening to the vibrations my feet make on the cliff, far above.

He's down there, waiting for me. He's been waiting for me all my life.

My foot slips and a fall of slate plummets twelve metres, sprinkling the surface and then vanishing. I step back. Someone is telling me to jump off a cliff. It's like a joke. No one jumps off a cliff just because someone has told them to. I'm not going to do it. It's only April; if I survived the fall the cold would kill me. I find myself sitting down. I rest my elbows on my knees and hold my head. If I jump, what then? Either I live or I die. If I live, does that mean Sheeley will be released? If I don't jump, does that mean she's going to be murdered? The idea is crazy, and yet, here I am. And her phone is dead. And HE had her ring. Can I risk it? And if I die, by, say, hitting my head on a rock, or dying of shock, what then? Will HE have seen? Will HE release Sheeley?

Is my life worth less than Sheeley's? What am I going to do with it anyway? Take over the scrapyard when Dad retires? Become a vulture, like him, picking up the parts from crashes?

I can't jump.

But kids have jumped off here before, and survived. That one that died, he was unlucky, everyone said. Other boys made it, one boy didn't. I still don't like the odds. I'm not a lucky person. I'm Scrappy. Maybe I should be someone else. I run through my cast. I can't think of anyone who would jump over this cliff, not Dad, not Silva, definitely not Judge. Only Scrappy would get himself into this kind of mess.

I hear Dad's voice in my head. "For God's sake, stop dithering," he says. "You're driving me mad."

I can't do it unless I shut my eyes.

I walk to the edge.

I can't do it.

BEEP BEEP.

It's another text. I don't read the message for some time. I can see the sun breaking through the clouds. I think I can hear a whispering in my ears. *Don't do it*. Or maybe I'm imagining it. It's hard to know what is real any more.

I read the message.

HER FATE IN UR HANDS.

"LEAVE ME ALONE," I scream, hurling the phone into

the quarry, and watch it fall and fall. Before it hits the water it's me, Scrappy, who runs over the edge and throws myself after it.

Water Snake

I smash into the water, feet first, and it feels like I've been punched. My shoes are torn off. I'm going down, down, into utter darkness. The cold is shocking and an intense pressure is squeezing my chest. I'm still going down, though I'm not sure which way is up any more. I must move, but everything hurts. The water is so heavy it's pressing me down. It's so dark. Blackness. How can water be black? I'm dead now. Surely? But it hurts; how can I be dead if it hurts? I open my eyes underwater. I see nothing. Nothing. There's nothing here.

No, there's something. Something is moving towards me. I'm slowing down. I'm hanging here. It's getting close to me, something awful. Not the snake. Please not the snake. The water has turned dark blue. I can see blurry shapes. There's something hanging in the water. It's caught up in some coils of rope. A body. Oh God, not Sheeley? It drifts in the cold currents, lolls round to greet me. A pale, pale face. It's not Sheeley. I scream underwater as he grins at me, his eyes black, black holes of emptiness. Cold water fills my chest, my lungs. I'm going down.

I'm coming up. I can't stop coughing. I'm coughing so much I can't breathe. My throat is burning. And I'm so cold. Now there's a voice, miles above me. I open my eyes. I'm shaking. I can see the sun through the clouds.

"Lunatic." Judge's face swims into focus.

But I'm alive! I did it!

"What did you do that for?" Judge pants. "I saw you. I *saw* you." He sits me up against a rock and roughly wraps his jacket around me. I'm so cold it hurts. I'm not wearing any socks. My feet look so pale and soft. Like a dead man's feet. Why do my arms ache?

"I had to drag you out," says Judge. "You're crazy." He's wet too, all except his coat. He had the sense to take it off before he rescued me. All of this must be his fault. My brain is clicking into place.

"Why did you go and do that?" Judge sits back on his haunches, looks at me. He looks grey and stupid. But my lungs hurt so I can't say anything. I cough and cough, burning coughs that rack my body. Judge is saying something to me but I don't know what. When I've stopped coughing, I gather my strength.

"Where's Sheeley?" I ask.

Judge looks surprised. "How in the hell should I know?"

He looks mad and scared. "You're insane, you are."

Judge is the one! Then I see a rifle propped up against a rock and I freeze. Fear trickles down my cold body. He's been carrying it with him all the time. That's what was in his tool bag.

"He's delirious," says Judge, talking to the sky. He frowns at me. "What made you do that?"

"Where's Sheeley?" I repeat. I can't take my eyes off the gun. I find it hard to believe that he really means to shoot me.

We're in the bottom of the quarry, sitting on the stones that slope down to the water. The cliffs tower above us. I can see Big Man, the ledge jutting out blackly in the morning light. I jumped from that. And I made it! Despite everything, I feel a surge of energy.

"You needn't look so bloody pleased with yourself," says Judge. "You'd have been a goner if I hadn't been here."

I pull my knees up to my chest and wrap his coat around me. It stinks of sweat.

"Was that a suicide attempt, Scrappy?" Judge asks.

"It was your idea, wasn't it?" I grunt.

I wonder if I can try and grab the gun and chuck it in the water, just to be on the safe side.

"Where is my sister?" I ask him again.

"Will you stop asking me questions I don't know?" he says. "And maybe answer some of mine."

"I saw something down there," I say, remembering as my head clears. I look at the water. Think about what's in it.

A clattering of stones above me draws me back to the surface. I'm filled with a sudden terror as I

189

recognize Louis, Judge's friend, making his way down to us. Why is he here?

This is it then.

I hug my knees. There's no use trying to run. I'm too weak.

"What's up?" shouts Louis, and his voice bounces off the water and echoes round the cliff.

They're going to shoot me. Judge is saying something but I don't hear. I'm only aware that I'm deadly tired, and so scared I'll do anything to survive. I eye up the gun. Anything.

"Did he get away?" calls Judge.

"He's long gone," replies Louis.

Are they talking about Grandad? Were they going to shoot him as well?

Judge looks at me. "Don't say anything about this, will you?" he says. "My dad will go mad if he finds out I've borrowed his gun."

"That's unlikely," I manage to stutter. I've got to get up, I've got to try and grab the gun and run before they shoot me like a rat.

I try to stand and to my amazement Judge helps me. "If I hadn't woken up and followed you up here, you would have drowned, I swear you would. Good job Louis wasn't late. And we wouldn't be here at all if it wasn't for the stag."

"What?"

"You must have seen him," says Judge. "He was up here just a few minutes ago. He crossed by your dad's yard. We've been after him for weeks now." Judge gestures to his gun. "Please don't tell anyone, though. We'd be dead. Dad thinks this gun is locked away."

"We've been following him on the internet," says Louis, clattering down to join us. "He's been hiding up around your quarry for the last two weeks. You didn't believe the bull about car parts, did you?"

I don't know what to think. Judge is stalking the stag? Not me?

"You were going to shoot him?" I gasp. "That's sick."

Judge shrugs. "No sicker than some of the stuff you get up to in your spare time. What made you jump off Big Man?" He looks suspicious. "Was it another text?"

My mind is slowly clearing.

"Why did you come with me to the show home?"

"To look for the stag," says Judge. "I don't really believe all this stuff about your sister. It's just some joker. This is real life, Scrappy. You've got an overactive imagination, which gets you into trouble."

"That's not what you said on the phone last night," says Louis, yawning and looking at his watch. "You were quite keen for me to come over, as I recall."

"You've been hunting the stag?" I repeat.

"There's hundreds of people hunting him," says Judge. "He's famous, isn't he? Been in the papers and on the radio. But now I find I'm caught up with your crazy stuff."

"So you haven't been sending me messages?"

"What, like a psychic? 'Course I bloody haven't. What would I do that for?"

This means Mr Mouse is still out there. I check my pockets for my phone before I remember I threw it in the quarry. At least that means no more messages.

But what about Sheeley?

I'm walking down the field behind Judge and Louis. Judge has got his gun in the bag slung over his shoulder. I didn't know he went out hunting but maybe that's a hobby you don't talk about. I'm barefoot. I picture my shoes, still slowly sinking into deeper, darker water. Some kind of self-preservation has prevented me from thinking too much about what I saw down there until now. I saw a body, a drowned body, but did I really? I could have been hallucinating, seeing things that aren't there with my stupid eyes. I don't remember getting to the surface, or Judge hauling me on to dry land. I must have lost consciousness. Now my feet are numb with cold, but I have no choice but to walk through the perishing grass. My wet clothes are rubbing against me. I struggle on, looking enviously at Judge's boots. He's a dark horse. If it hadn't been for him, would I have drowned? Did Judge save my life?

I can hear Petal barking. She's going crazy. I imagine her yanking at her rope, and frothing at the mouth. She must be thirsty. Down in the valley, the cars pound the road. People are going about their nice, warm business like everything is normal. But it isn't.

Where are my family?

We're nearly there but I have to sit down. I rub my feet, trying to get some blood back into them. In the end Judge and Louis each put one of my arms over their shoulders, and help me down the field and into the yard.

Olly is waiting for me, his hands on his hips. His grizzled old face is confused and angry. Without asking why I am soaking wet and being half carried down the hillside, he launches into the offensive.

"Who's been driving Thomas's car? And why did I find Ted trapped in the plane? He couldn't get past the dog. What's going on?"

"Where's Grandad?" I manage to ask.

"I took him back to the cottage. He kept going on about ghosts and Geebos. What have you been up to, Michael? Where is Thomas? And who are these clowns?" He glowers at Judge and Louis.

Judge, however, being Judge, isn't one bit afraid of Olly. "Have you got hold of your sister yet?" he asks, as if Olly isn't even there.

I shake my head and look away. I don't want Judge to see the tears starting in my eyes.

"What is all this about Sheeley?" asks Olly, concern clouding his face. He's got a soft spot for Sheeley. We all do.

I look between them all, not knowing who to trust or what to say. One of them has to be behind all this. But right now I just want to go home and get warm. I'll die of hypothermia if I stay out here one more minute.

Pushing past the three of them, I stumble over the yard. This is pain. My feet are red and raw and stinging. I curl up my toes and hobble. "Ouch, ouch, bloody ouch," I howl. I even consider crawling up to the flat. Look at me, I lose my shoes and I'm helpless. Finally I reach the garage. I grab the spare key from under a brick by the wall and let myself in, locking the door behind me. The stair carpet feels wonderfully soft under my feet. I'm home! I made it!

When I'm upstairs, I look out of the window and see Judge, Louis and Olly talking in the yard, all casting glances up at the flat. I try to think what Judge knows. He was there when I got the message about Sheeley. That's why he's here. He's telling Olly. And I did it, I jumped off Big Man. Mr Mouse has always kept his side of the bargain up till now. I've done what's right for Sheeley. But right now I can't do anything until I get warm. I strip off my wet things and run myself a bath.

The hot water stings as I lower myself in. My feet are grimy and covered in scratches. The warmth washes over me as I sink lower. I feel myself relaxing and my heart seems to beat slower. The bathroom is full of steam. The events of the last twenty-four hours are flying round my head. I have to piece it all together but everything happened so fast it was hard to take it all in. My eyelids feel heavy and hot. I could shut my eyes, just for a minute. I could make my mind go blank and forget all the madness. I need to shut down.

I snap my eyes open and sit up in the bath. I saw

it – the thing in the quarry water. I saw the awful featureless face. I'm still trying to convince myself it was a dream, but deep down, I know it was not. It was real. It was a drowned body.

There's banging on the door downstairs. I'd better let them in. But as I'm heaving myself out of the bath the phone rings. I grab a towel and stumble into the hallway to answer it. I desperately want it to be Dad, or Sheeley, or Mum. But when I pick up the phone I swear my hair stands on end when I hear this nasty rasping breathing. A horrible crawling feeling travels up my back.

"*April Fool*," says a voice before the phone goes dead.

April Fool

I let the receiver fall to the floor. It was him. Mr Mouse actually spoke to me. I stare at the phone for a few seconds. I didn't recognize the voice. It was a man with no obvious accent. I pick up the receiver and dial 1471 but the number is withheld. I'm trying to work out what to do next but it's hard to think with the hammering on the door downstairs. I'm going to have to let them in.

April Fool.

I pull on a dry jumper and jeans and go down. Olly stands by the door; his ugly face is a mass of worry. Judge and Louis are lurking by the office. Why don't they go home? I'm shivering again. I feel as helpless as a worm.

"You have some talking to do," says Olly, hooking his thumbs into his jeans. "Your pal there has been talking about you getting threats."

"Come on," I say wearily, gesturing him inside. Judge hurries over to join him. I'm too weak to argue so I let him in too. But even before we get upstairs they're firing questions at me.

"Where's Sheeley?" Olly demands. "Is it true about the threats?"

My head is spinning. I keep seeing *that* face.

"He *says* the threats are real," says Judge.

"I'm not making it up," I say. We're in the sitting room but no one wants to sit.

"I'm the last person to call on the law in usual circumstances, but in this case I think you should," says Olly. I don't think Olly's ever been in the flat, and he's been working for Dad for ever. He shifts from one foot to the other and is making a point of not standing on the rug.

"I got a call just now," I say, flexing my aching arm. "I think it was *him*. He said *April Fool*."

"I'm phoning the police, now," says Olly. "And then you must phone Thomas." But as he gets his mobile out, the phone in the hall rings again. What now?

RING RING.

We look at each other. I can't move. I don't want to play this any more.

RING RING.

It's madness, I know, but I can't help thinking that the thing I saw down in the quarry water and the voice on the phone are the same thing. I'm too scared to answer. I watch helplessly as Olly gives a grunt and snatches up the receiver.

"Yes," he says, in his deep old voice. "Olly. Well hello," he says, his voice full of surprise. He leans into the doorway and gives me the thumbs up. Me, I'm rooted to the spot. "He's had a busy morning," he says, casting an odd look at me. He doesn't seem like a man who's talking to a ghost. "He's here," says Olly. "Would you like a word?" He holds out the receiver, pulling it so hard the phone nearly comes off the wall and the base dangles in the air.

I stare at it dumbly. I can't move the metre to the doorway. "Come on, I've wasted enough time already today," orders Olly. Somehow I get to the door, and take the phone.

"The boy is terrified," mutters Olly. "It's all right, lad," he says to me. Then he shakes his head and walks down the hall to the stairs. "I'm going home now, but I'll be telling your dad about this morning," he says.

I press the receiver to my ear. "Hello?" I croak.

"HAPPY BIRTHDAY!"

Sheeley.

SHEELEY! I'm so relieved I want to cry. I can't say anything for a few minutes but listen as she gabbles on about coming round later and how her phone charger has gone missing, but she's spoken to Dad and he'll be back later with a new grab for Bella he's been tracking with Jimmy, and how she's put a deposit down on a house in town. "A real house, with a garden."

"Where are you?" I finally manage. She's "at Donna's". She's "so much better". When she finally hangs up, I turn to face Judge.

"Your sister?" he says.

I nod, still unable to believe it.

"Well, that's good," he says. "You almost had me worried there." But then his face hardens. "You're a freak, Scrappy," he says. He's back to himself now. It's like he's grown a film over him. We are back to the usual status quo. "Did you make all this up?"

"No!" I say. But I'm so tired, so paranoid that I'm beginning to wonder. Am I going mad? I've been getting *messages*. Classic nut job. I've said before that if people whisper that you're mad, it can be hard to prove them wrong. But once you start to think your own self is mad, well, that's an even harder thought to get rid of.

"I'm going," says Judge. He makes for the door; then, as an afterthought: "Don't do anything stupid."

A few minutes later Petal is barking her distinctive farewell. Someone has tied her up again. I hear the clink of the gate. He's gone.

The next half-hour is like being awake in a dream. There are the usual noises.

WOOF   WOOF   WOOF   wheeesttttttts, wheeeeeeeeeestt WOOF WOOF. The same blurry view; the grey sky, the motorway; all my usual home comforts. As for me, I feel light-headed and wobbly. I feel like I'm being watched; I'm watching *myself*. Maybe I banged my head on the way down. I'm not hungry but I know I should eat. It's what normal people do. Normal people eat, go to the bog, and sleep. I will do these things. I look at the counter and see I've already made myself some toast and jam, but the toast has gone cold. I boil the kettle for tea and find the milk carton standing in the middle of the floor. I don't remember putting it there. I go back to the window, cradling my mug. It's lukewarm now; how did that happen? I look down over the yard, past Petal's van and the ring fence, down the lane and over to the roundabout. Cars are flying round. Further down the motorway booms, the vehicles pulsing up and down. My reflection sits on the glass like a ghost. It's Scrappy, nobody else. I stand and stare until my eyes sting.

When the letter box rattles, I startle. The mail claps on the tiles in the porch. I see the postman drive off, hunkering down in his seat against the cold. I follow myself down the stairs, over the red swirls. Normal, sane people pick up the post, so that's what I do too.

It's a big pile, lying higgledy piggledy, and amongst the brown bills there are splashes of colour. A yellow envelope and a purple one too and a cream one with a dirty fingerprint on, like the postman slipped in the mud and scattered the mail. And all of these colours are for me. I recognize the handwriting on the yellow one, scratched out like it was written by someone with claws. That's from Grandma, down in Cornwall. She never comes to see us because she doesn't like Dad. I sort through the others. The purple one is from Aunty Sarah. All from relations, none from friends. Boys don't give each other birthday cards, only girls do that. I don't bother opening them. I'm past caring about pictures of footballs and soppy poems. I'm not even bothered to find a sly tenner tucked away in amongst the birthday greetings. I'm looking for something else. But instead I hear a faint scratching, coming from the wall above me. I tilt my head to look and see a hard-cased insect, as fat as my thumb, creep up the wall, twitching its feelers.

"Hello again," I whisper. "Back from the dead."

They did say it was hard to kill a cockroach. And here's my little pal, scuttling through the fallout. And here is the other thing. It's sitting quiet and innocent under a shiny tool catalogue; a manila envelope with my name on.

Mr Mouse still hasn't finished with me.

Boy Missing

The carpet on the bottom tread is more worn than the rest, as if people start to come upstairs, then change their minds. I sit here and slit open the envelope. I had hoped, seeing as how I'd just hurled myself off a cliff for this person, it might have all come to a head and things might start slowing down. Especially now my mobile is gathering silt in the bottom of the quarry. But Mr Mouse still has plans for me. There's a lined piece of paper inside, torn from a pad. Also a small folded newspaper cutting, yellow with age or something else. I read the note first.

Is he still there?

Mr Mouse knows about the body in the quarry. Maybe he knows how it got there too.

"Yes," I say aloud like the freak I am. "He is, he is. He's coming apart, but he's still there all right." I read on.

The shot tower. Today. Don't you want to know who I am?

I breathe out, long and slow through my nostrils, rub my face. My hands must be still cold from the quarry because they're shaking. I need a clear head to think about all this, but there's no likelihood of getting one of those. I unfold the newspaper clipping. It's dated twenty years ago. June twenty-first.

I read the headline.

BOY MISSING IN QUARRY. FEARED DROWNED.

I look at the picture. It's a copy of a school photo. The hair has been brushed but a bit sticks up at the front. The teeth look too big for the face. There are a few spots on the chin. The mouth grins like he means it. This is the dead boy, then. It is him, of course. This is horrible but I read on. It's only a short paragraph, like the boy isn't important enough to justify more words.

A local boy, age 16, is missing, possibly after jumping into Gaunston Quarry. Two pairs of shoes were found at the top of the cliff, on the high peak known locally as "Big Man". One set of shoes has been confirmed as belonging to David Winkleigh. No one has identified the second pair. Police divers have searched the water, but say it is impossible to reach the greatest depths. The evidence suggests another person also jumped with David. Witnesses say they saw several boys making their way to the quarry that evening. None have come forward. Police believe

David may have become trapped in submerged plant machinery. They are appealing for witnesses.

"Well, OK, Mr Mouse," I say. "I'll come and meet you."

I'm still watching myself. I am performing for an audience of none. If I go to the shot tower, I'll see him. Or I'll see someone else. Or I'll find nothing at all and soon after get another cryptic message. When does this all stop and why has he sent me a clipping about the drowned boy?

I force myself through the motions again, doing my normal-person things. I put on a warm fleece. I eat a bowl of cereal. I heat myself a can of beans and eat them out of the pan with the wooden spoon. I pee and wash my face. But I still don't feel ready. I feel awful. A sick feeling in my stomach rolls back and forth like waves.

The shot tower has got scaffolding all round it at the moment. The authorities are worried that all the flooding has weakened its foundations. They're doing tests on it to see how safe it is.

I guess I'm going to find that out.

I drink a tall glass of water. I tie my shoes. I can't go. I still feel too weak. I've had enough for one morning. I kick off my shoes again and find myself walking into my bedroom. I'm sitting on the bed. I'm pulling the duvet over my head. I breathe in the smell of me. I curl up in a ball. First I shut out Petal's barking (somebody needs to feed her), then I blank out the motorway music. Then I forget about stags and quarries and messages and try to think of nothing. I'm almost there when it appears. That face. The boy, David. I can't shut him out. I could have joined him. Maybe I'm next. Mr Mouse wanted history to repeat itself! My head is swirling and whirling with increasingly mad thoughts. I wish I was out of it.

I open my eyes. My room is gloomy with half-arsed daylight. I fell asleep! But I couldn't have climbed the shot tower earlier. I'd have fallen off and died. According to my digital alarm clock I've been asleep for four hours, as it is one o'clock in the afternoon. I'm muzzy-headed but the memories of the last twenty-four hours clear my brain like a drench of cold water. I scoop myself out of bed to check the yard. No cars. I'm alone.

Let's look at this logically. I'm going to climb a dangerous tower to find someone who hates me. That's stupid. But I already crossed the line when I jumped off Big Man. Anyway, I'm not going to get up there and meekly take whatever next evil plan Mr Mouse has in store for me. I'm going to smash his bloody face in. I'm strong now. I've slept and eaten. My sister is safe. I'm sixteen years old. I'm six feet tall and no weakling. HE is bloody going to get it for messing me around. I'm not scared any more. The anger is building up in me, bit by bit. It is rage which powers me down the stairs and out of the door.

I grab my bicycle and drag it through the mud. I pass

Petal, and when she rushes out to snarl and growl I get an overwhelming urge to run over and kick her.

"SHUT UP!" I scream so loudly my throat hurts.

Anger fills me and I am going towards her when I stop. She cringes back, expecting the worst. Instead of kicking the horrible thing, I go over and unclip her lead from the chain.

"Now can you STOP BARKING?" I yell.

I expect her to run off into the fields but instead she scampers into the bushes. Despite everything I get a surge of amusement when Jasper comes flying out, his tail fat and his claws splayed. He climbs up on to a pile of cars and Petal stands at the bottom barking furiously.

"You've met your Waterloo, mate," I tell Jasper, making no attempt to rescue him. But he reminds me of Grandad, who I haven't seen all day.

I'm pedalling hard as I can, bouncing over bumps and flying round corners. My legs ache and my head is full of crap. I've got Petal running beside me on a rope. She's confused. She doesn't get taken for walks very often, but I want her with me.

"Slow down!"

I stop at the end of the lane and turn to watch as Grandad wobbles up, almost purple with the effort, on the pink racer Sheeley got for her thirteenth birthday.

"This isn't what I meant when I said I wanted to go out for a ride," he pants.

He's switched on today. When I said I needed him to

come with me, because someone had been hassling me, he was out of the door before I was. I don't know how much use he'll be. But I need some kind of backup.

"I haven't ridden one of these things for years," says Grandad.

I'm glad I've got him and Petal with me. Team Scrappy vs Mr Mouse.

It's mostly downhill to Gaunston. I usually manage it in twenty minutes, but I have to slow the pace for Grandad and Petal, neither of whom are very fit. Instead of going to the shot tower, I find myself leading us to the other side of town, where the houses are old and big and have flower beds and garden paths. I leave my bike, Petal and Grandad at the bottom of the path and run and bang on Silva's door. There are pots of yellow flowers either side of it. I can't take my eyes off them. They're so bright and cheerful. They're crazy flowers.

Kennett opens the door and looks at me blankly. He's wearing an old green suit that's too small for him. It's got a long yellow smear down one side. The confusion lifts from his face and his eyes narrow.

"Scrappy," he says. "I didn't recognize you. Are you all right?"

"Yeah," I say, in a thick voice that doesn't sound like mine.

Kennett watches me. He takes a step closer and peers at my eyes. I stare back. "Come in," he says. "You look like you need a sit-down."

"No," I say. "I just need to see Silva."

"So come in," he repeats. He looks worried. "Are you in trouble, Michael? Can I help?"

"I just need to see Silva."

Kennett sighs. "I wish you'd come in."

I stare at the ground. I'm going to have to go if he keeps this up.

"All right." Kennett steps inside, leaving the door wide open. I see the wide hall and beyond it, the kitchen. The table is covered with toy cars and felt pens. I turn round and look at the garden instead. Silva is taking his time. I can hear voices from inside, but can't make out what they're saying.

Finally he appears. "What's going on? The old man thinks you're on drugs?"

If it was funny I'd laugh.

"I'm not on drugs. I'm just freaked out."

Silva looks behind me and closes the door. He steps towards me, puts a hand on my arm. On one hand, his nails are short, for fingering the fretboard on his guitar; on the other hand his nails are long, for plucking the strings. I have the long-nailed hand on my arm.

"I'm being stalked," I say. "I've got to do something. I need you to be there. I've got to go now."

And Silva doesn't look at me like I'm mad or messed up. "Are you going to tell me anything else?" he asks.

"On the way," I say. "I'm in a rush." Because now I'm worried that Mr Mouse will think I'm not coming and won't be there any more.

Silva glances back at the house. "Is it dodgy, man?"

he asks. "Should I write my will?"

"I just need you to wait," I say. "Please."

Silva sticks his head round the door and calls out something I don't bother to tune into and then he's with me, having extracted his own bike from somewhere.

"Mystery man," he mutters. "I knew something was up with you. You've been more offish than usual. Still, this is better than telly. Oh." He stops dead when he sees Petal and Grandad, now sitting in the hedge.

"Hello, Mr Singer," he says, stepping sideways to avoid Petal's snarl. "What are you doing in there?"

"Keeping dry," says Grandad. "Call me Ted." He looks at me. "I'm tired, Michael." And he rubs his big old purple nose. I shouldn't have brought him with me but I didn't want to leave him at home.

Silva looks at us, thinking.

"Do you want to come and have a cup of tea with my old man, Ted?" he asks. "We've got a cake somewhere, I'm sure."

"Yes," says Grandad. "Only. . ." He looks at me. "Wasn't there something you needed me for?"

"I'll be fine," I say.

"But I'm afraid Petal might alarm my pet dinosaur," says Silva, eyeing her.

"She's coming with us," I say.

I don't know what Silva said to Kennett, but whatever it was, it worked, and Silva says Grandad is now lodged in front of the TV with a mug of tea and a whole packet

209

of biscuits. It's a relief. We're on our bikes now, riding two abreast. I don't know how to explain everything to Silva.

"Am I, like your henchman?" asks Silva, whizzing along beside me with his arms folded. "Because if you want me to fight someone – is it Judge? – can I nip back and get my kung fu manual?"

"I don't need you to protect me," I say angrily. "I need you to protect *him*."

Shot Tower

We cycle through town. It's hard to believe it's a normal Saturday for most people. We ride over the town bridge and the river runs fast and brown, pooling over the banks where they haven't sorted out the flood defences. We pass the school. The playing field has turned into a lake, rippling in the wind. I imagine fish swimming through the goalposts, nibbling the nets. There's water everywhere and the wet is creeping up my jeans. Petal's become this tired, nervous old dog, definitely not the lunatic hellhound I'm used to. I've never taken her into town before and she keeps shying away from the cars and sniffing the ground as we move.

When we reach the old industrial estate we abandon our bikes. Silva locks his, I don't bother. We squeeze through the gap at the end of the metal fencing into the disused car park. The lower part of the car park is flooded, and the shot tower stands in about a metre of dirty water. It's about twenty metres high and wrapped all round with scaffolding and plastic. I can't see any life up there. There are no cars in the car park, no smell of cigarette smoke. No clues at all. Just the grey sky and the tower, and me and Silva, standing like lemons. I'm feeling calm now, calm and determined. I want to end this.

Silva touches my shoulder. "Scrappy, it's time to talk. What is this madness?"

"I've got to go up," I say.

"Dad was right, you are on drugs," he says. "Don't be stupid. You'd fall. Anyway, why?"

"For a dare," I reply.

I take a deep breath and tell him about Mr Mouse and the messages. I tell him about the cockroaches, the chickens, the date and how I was supposed to fight Judge. Silva doesn't interrupt when I tell him about Sheeley and the show home. I can feel the anger growing in me again. Then I tell him about Big Man, about *April Fool*.

"You jumped into the quarry?" Silva's eyes are wide. "Today?"

But I don't want to talk any more. I'm off, running over the concrete before I change my mind. Petal bounds behind me, trailing her rope.

"But this is just another dare," shouts Silva. "You're playing into his hands."

"He's up there," I pant.

"Scrappy, this is twisted." Silva is beside me, pulling at my arm. "It's like you're being made to go through some kind of rites. You've had to steal something, kill something, fight someone, pull a girl, be a hero. What's

212

he going to do to you this time? Scrappy, don't do it. Walk away."

"I can't stand it any more. I've got to end it," I say.

"That's what I'm worried about," says Silva.

We're splashing at the foot of the tower. I find a big, locked door which doesn't budge even when I boot it. The scaffolding towers above us. There's a big gap between the ground and the first rung.

"I dare you *not* to go up," pants Silva. "No one's watching except me."

Oh, he's watching. I know that.

"And what exactly am I supposed to do when you fall off?" demands Silva. "I haven't got a mop."

I'm going to meet him. I can sense him. It's like there's a heat coming from the top of the tower.

"Are you going to throw yourself off the top?" says Silva brightly. "Because that could mess up my exams, you know. Though not as much as yours."

"I'm not going to fall off," I shout back and I jump and grab the lower bar. I slip off, burning my fingers. I jump again, grab the bar and swing my legs up. I hook them round the metal tube. Then I pull myself up. I'm sweating already, but I tell myself this must be the hardest bit. I can see up through gaps in the planks and there are some ladders stacked a few platforms above. Petal watches me, her head on one side.

"I hope he doesn't ask you to kill your best friend," Silva mutters. "That would be a challenge to pass up, I hope. You're not really going to leave me down here with the Hound of the Baskervilles, are you?"

I climb up the outside of the scaffolding to the next level. It's not as hard as I thought. The only real danger is if my fingers slip off the wet bars. I wait for a minute to get my breath back. Through the gaps in the planking I see Silva, peering upwards.

"What are you expecting to find at the top?" he calls. "Is it a beautiful woman?"

I smile through gritted teeth. Silva's banter is calming me down, making me feel less murderous. I'm not stopping, though. Once I reach the ladders it is fairly straightforward for me to progress. I position the ladder and climb to the next stage, hauling it up after me. I'm trying not to think about anything except not falling off. I repeat the process, over and over, until I reach the top of the scaffold. The wind buffets me and I lean against the tower for support. The town is like an island, rising out of the water. I see the river thundering down the valley, spreading out over its banks. It's like a massive vertebrae dividing the land, with ribs of water pouring out from it. I see a crowd of cows in a field. They're standing in the one corner which isn't flooded. They nose at the water like it's alive.

The clouds darken. I feel rain on my cheek.

The scaffolding stops maybe four metres from the top. There's a window and it's open. A lip runs round the tower. This means I can no longer use the ladder but it's broad enough to swing myself up. I manage it without too many heebie-jeebies. I'm a long way up now. If I slipped, I might land on the scaffolding, but that's not exactly comforting. There's no railing on the top platform. I might bounce off.

Far below, the water ripples on the car park. A headache thumps behind my eyes. I shift my weight on the narrow ledge. I'm desperate for extra centimetres but everything is slippery with rain and I'm scared. My fingers are rubbed raw and my breath forces its way in and out of me. I make myself look up and rain drives into my face. There's so far to go, at least three metres before I reach the window. I don't know if I'm going to make it. But I can't let go. I haul myself up, stabbing the surface with my toes, forcing a way in. The wind is stronger and the rain comes at me harder. My foot slips and scrabbles against bare blocks. Adrenaline floods through me but as I brace for the fall, I miraculously find a new toehold.

How did I get here?

Don't think. Just climb.

I move again. Everything hurts. I feel like I'm holding on by my fingertips. Finally my fingers splay out over the lip below the window. Then my fingers find the ledge and curl over it like a vice.

"You've done it." Silva's voice is faint. "Well done, now come down." I can see him below, a matchstick man in a giant puddle.

I force myself onwards. My left leg threatens to cramp, as, screaming with effort, I force my aching body over the lip. I lie flat on my stomach on the ledge, the rain hammering into my back. I've made it. I've beaten my way to the top. I raise my head and look in through the window. For a dizzying moment, I feel like I am about to roll off and fall into oblivion.

But I don't fall. Instead, I slither over the window ledge and collapse into the interior, landing hard in a dark, circular room on a concrete floor. I lie panting and shaking for just a moment before I force myself to sit up. I wipe grit and salt water out of my eyes and taste blood on my tongue. As my eyes get used to the dark I see I'm in a low-ceilinged room right at the top of the tower. There is a wide circular hole in the floor, covered with a kind of mesh, coppery with rust. A low wall runs round the hole. The floor is scattered with chips of wood, pigeon crap, plaster debris and bits of old machinery. Rain blows in through the broken windows.

"What took you so long?"

The voice comes from the far side of the room.

"Oh God," I say as the figure sitting opposite swirls into focus. "Not you. Anyone but you."

Mr Mouse

"I thought you weren't coming."

Dad, *Dad* is sitting, no, *crouching,* in a metal chair. He's got his elbows on his knees, and his chin resting on his knuckles. I didn't recognize him at first because he's cut his hair off. It lies in a thick prickly pile by his chair. I stare and stare, my anger turning into total bewilderment.

"You look *mad,*" is all I can splutter. "Your hair. . ."

"Time for a change," says the man who is my dad but doesn't look like him any more.

He's got a massive bald spot above his forehead, with hair tufting out all around it.

Dad sees me looking and fingers the space.

"It's where I'm hottest," he says in a voice I don't recognize at all, and I feel the first pinching of terror.

"You climbed up but I took the stairs," he says gesturing. "I changed the locks."

I find it hard to take my eyes off him but quickly look over to a trapdoor in the floor.

"Dad?" My chest feels so tight I can hardly breathe. *Dad?*

"So did you see him?" Dad puts his hand over his eyes. "I see him all the bloody time."

My face feels like it is collapsing. My own dad did all this to me.

"David," prompts Dad. "Did you see David in the quarry?"

I'm wrenched back into the cold, cold water. I see the floating outline of a long-dead body, held together by its clothing. "Yeah," I croak. "I saw him."

Dad sighs a deep, bitter sigh. "I killed him," he says softly.

Outside, the scaffold creaks in the wind and the rain drives down. The room seems to fall away from us. It's just him and me. His face appears enormous: the loose skin, the big features, the deep wrinkles and this new, horrible exposed scalp.

"Plenty of kids jumped. We all did it. No one ever died. I knew you wouldn't either. This proves it wasn't my fault."

Dad's got a mess of stubble over his face. I see his mobile phone and a pair of binoculars at his feet. Mum gave him those binoculars for Christmas!

It's my dad up here! It's not Judge. It's my own dad!

"Why did you do it?" I ask him. "You're bloody mad. You could have killed me." I pick myself up off the floor. "That stuff about Sheeley, how could you?"

Dad grunts. "I didn't think money would be enough," he says. "And I needed you to do it. All of it. I don't want you ending up like me. I want you to do something with your life. Until all this started you spent every waking hour sat on your teenage arse reading books."

I stare at him. He's the mad one. Not me. He's Mr Mouse.

"I've done so much for you, for this family," says Dad. "And you just lie around like a bloody parasite."

I bite my tongue.

"You still don't get it, do you?" Dad peeks through a gap in his fingers. The bags under his eyes are enormous. "I've been doing you a favour. You've had more fun these last weeks than you've had in your entire life. I've shaken you up. It's what you needed too."

"I could have been killed jumping in the quarry," I say.

"But I knew you wouldn't. I *knew* it was safe." Dad's almost pleading with me now. "And I needed to know David was there. *He wanted me to find him.*"

"Then why the hell didn't you jump in yourself?" I snarl.

"I couldn't," Dad says. "I couldn't because he would be waiting for me. He's got nothing against you."

"What are you talking about?"

"He wouldn't jump," says Dad. "So I pushed him. It was just a laugh. I jumped in after him. Only when I came up, he didn't."

I stare and stare at him.

"He's been quiet for years," says Dad. "But these last

few months I see his face everywhere. He's on my tail, Mikey. He won't leave me alone."

"Does Mum know?" I ask in a shaky voice.

"Of course she does, she was there too," he snaps. "Only now she wants to clear everything up. She wants to find his parents, tell them what really happened. She says she couldn't bear it if it was you, disappearing like that, and never finding the body. Never knowing for sure."

"But why now, after all this time?" I ask. "I thought it happened years ago."

Dad uncurls himself from his chair and stands. I step back as he jiggles the mesh covering the hole with his boot. "It's because you're sixteen. That's how old we were, when. . ." He pauses. "When the accident happened. Cat says she's not going to cover for me any more because it's driving her mad." Dad gives an odd sort of laugh. "I'll testify to that. Now, for God's sake, get this thing finished with. Tell the police you fell in and found him. Get him brought up and buried. That's what he wants. He doesn't want to be down there any more."

I disregard the madness in his words, that he knows what a dead boy does or doesn't want. Instead I try and focus on what is real. "But Dad, how did you know I'd find him when all those police divers didn't?" For the first time today, Dad looks at me head on. His eyes are stricken.

"He's come back, Mikey," he says quietly. "He's

started coming to me, night after night. I shut my eyes and I see his face. I can't sleep. It's getting worse." Dad's voice is so quiet I can barely hear him. "He's always messed with me. He turns lights off, hides keys, breaks the generator. He writes things on my computer. He's driven the bloody dog mad. But now he's showing himself. All this rain, it's saturated the ground. Things are coming to the surface which have been buried for years."

He rubs his scalp. "You needed a good shaking up anyway, Michael."

"You did it again," I say, flaring up. "You pushed David over and you pushed me too."

"It was safe," whispers Dad. "Lots of us jumped. We did it all the time. That's what kids did those days, but David got wrapped around something."

"But why drag me into it?" I say.

The man in front of me sucks in his breath. "I had to prove to *him* that it wasn't my fault. I had to show him it was safe, really."

I try to get my head round Dad's logic. He made me, his son, jump because he wanted to prove that it was *safe*? To a *dead* boy? I'm feeling this sickening feeling, a deep, deep horror about what my dad really is.

Everything makes sense now.

"You're mad," I say, and my voice sounds panicky.

Dad bends and rubs his feet. "Pins and needles," he says to me and grins this awful grin. He straightens. "You will go to the police, and tell them what you saw.

Tell them where to find David. Don't say anything about me. Then he can be laid to rest." Dad looks over his shoulder. "Then maybe he'll leave me alone."

The rain blows in through the window, making a puddle on the floor. Me, I'm a mess. I don't know where to go from here. I've been betrayed. Your dad is supposed to back you up. He's not supposed to hound you until you think you're going mad.

Dad takes a step towards me. "Please, Michael," he says.

I'm scared now. I feel cold and weak. This isn't my dad, this is someone new. He walks round the mesh in the floor to me and puts a hand on my shoulder. "We were only playing, weren't we?"

"Get off me." I push him and he steps back.

He stares at me. I swear his eyes have changed. There's someone else behind them, someone else driving him.

I've got to get out of here.

"Goodbye, Mikey," Dad says blankly and he steps back and stamps into the mesh screen covering the shot hole.

"No! Dad!" I scream in terror as the thing is wrenched from its moorings and Dad plummets into the darkness. The last thing I see is the whites of his eyes.

Now it has to be over. It's too far to fall and survive. "Dad?"

And now it ought to be quiet, but it's not. I can hear something, him, scuffling in the darkness below, and I creep over, sick with fear, and peer into the gloom and as I look a shape begins to appear and it is a man, maybe ten metres down, and he is stuck fast like a fly in a web. I can see more now; he's wedged in a lower mesh screen. His shoulder and hip have punched through but the rest of him hasn't.

The noise of his breathing rises to meet me.

"Dad?"

Scrappy

I've been living with Silva's family since it all happened. Kennett and Becky say it's no problem and I can stay as long as I like. Kennett says what's one more mouth? And anyway Silva's eldest sister has just moved in with Sheeley in her new place so there's a bit more space. I've even been doing a bit of paperwork for Kennett. He's almost as disorganized as Dad was. Time has passed quickly. I feel as if I've been in a daze for weeks. I've done my exams and finished school – and school is finished. It is now three mountains of red and grey rubble and the air is full of dust. Silva says this school dust will make us brainy if we breathe it in.

Dad is ill, really, deeply ill. Lots of people have known this for years: Mum, Olly, Grandad. Not me and Sheeley, though I guess we had our suspicions. But how are we supposed to know what is normal? We grew up with Thomas Singer. We didn't have any other dad. He wasn't ill. To me, he just had *characteristics*. Like his erratic temper. Like sleeping in his office, being a workaholic, like sometimes vanishing for weeks on end. Mum looked after him, soothed him, and kept him going.

But when she left, he flipped. Now he's been certified and he's in a secure hospital eighty kilometres away. Sheeley got a phone call from him. Dad said he felt like he'd been in a deep pit, but now there was a ladder. He's never said stuff like this before so maybe the hospital is doing him some good.

My dad.

It all makes sense now I look back on it. I don't know if I am sad or relieved. I think maybe both. I'm not missing him yet. What I do miss is my family. I haven't visited Dad yet. Me and Sheeley might go together sometime. We haven't decided.

After what happened, lots of people came to talk to us. The police came. People came to talk to Grandad and to me. And I told them about David.

Isn't it amazing how families can keep the hugest secrets from each other, for years and years? But when these festering secrets eventually get discovered, winkled out like a fossilized dinosaur, the world is never the same again. That's what my dad's secret was like: a sleeping dinosaur.

But then it woke up and ate him alive.

I've remembered something recently. It was about ten years ago. I was five or six, and I was walking down our lane with Mum. I was holding her hand and we were chatting. It was a warm, bright afternoon. I had a red ice lolly. I think Sheeley was spending the day with friends, so it was just me and Mum. The juice from the lolly was running down my hands and I was licking it off, when something jumped out at us from the hedge. Not a stag this time, but a man, a tall, shouting man. I was so surprised I dropped the lolly. Mum screamed and screamed and kept going even when it was perfectly obvious it was only Dad. He'd jumped out to scare us. A trick. A joke. But Mum started crying and then Dad stormed off. I don't remember thinking it odd. I was only annoyed that I'd ruined my lolly. Funny how I'd forgotten that until now.

On the afternoon of the burial I hung around with Silva. We sat in the shade of the big old oak at the bottom of the town playing fields and watched the time. The water had all dried up and the grass was growing back, but there were still muddy slicks here and there. There were traces of the flood all over town, even then, months later: dead trees, traffic cones in strange places and abandoned sandbags. The park was still a mess. A smell of drains and stagnant water lingered. It was as if the edges had blurred between wet and dry.

We could see the church on the hill above us. The service was at two o'clock. We weren't going. Mum asked me to go with her but I suggested she take Sheeley instead. It was David's funeral, twenty years late.

A figure appeared at the end of the path and walked

over to us. He flopped on the ground next to me, pulled his cap over his eyes.

"Hey, Judge," I said.

We sat under the tree and waited until we saw the people coming out of the church. Four figures carried David's coffin and then others filed out, in twos and threes, into the churchyard and up behind some trees. We waited in silence. I lay back and looked up at the leaves above, shimmering and blowing. I felt so strange and sad. I never knew David, but now I see how the tragedy of his death has shaped and twisted my life.

I sat up when Silva nudged me. Cars were driving away down the hill.

It was over.

And Grandad, what about Grandad? Here's the thing. I don't want to look after him all the time, but I don't want to abandon him either. This is why, one week after David's funeral, Kennett has driven him up here from the old people's home. I still see him. He's got worse. Sometimes he remembers who I am. Sometimes he doesn't. Sometimes he pretends he knows who I am, which is even more confusing. I don't know if he's happier or not; the only thing he's clear about is the food. He says the cooking is much better than mine.

Today, though, he's clear and lucid and we're back at his favourite place. Somewhere we still come to quite a lot. Somewhere we have work to do.

I can't say *Happy Ted's* has improved under its new

ownership, though I do notice that Petal is no longer kept in the transit. Today I find her curled up on the back seat of Olly's jeep. She gives me a cursory snarl but it's nothing compared to her usual standards. Olly steps out from behind the bonnet.

"She likes it better being able to run around," he says by way of greeting.

Petal looks better; her teeth look brighter and her coat has a shine. There's more flesh on her.

Although the cottage is up for rent, Olly has taken over the yard and flat. I must say he's looking perky. He's bought himself a new baseball cap and had a haircut. He's had a major clear-out. He's installed CCTV. Whatever. The main thing is that he doesn't mind me and Grandad coming here to play our games, to live our dreams.

We sit in the cockpit of the Fokker. I'm the co-pilot. Imagine if, when Grandad flipped the ignition switches, the engine fired into life. The gas is compressed and drawn into the turbine. Imagine those propellers whizzing round and round. I can feel the old plane shudder. Grandad can feel it too. Just think how loud it would be. We'd look at each other in delight as the roar filled our ears. Then see how we'd move, brambles snapping as the old bird broke free, steering slowly over the concrete yard. The shadows of the wings ripple over the grey garage walls. Imagine us bump into the field, turn the corner and start to run downhill. Imagine us picking up speed, going faster, faster, faster.

Imagine us belting through the gateway, the wings clipping the top of the hedge either side. Imagine us going as fast as falling down the field towards the cut. Now see him pull the yoke and then feel the lift under the wings. Hear the clatter as the broken wheel mechanism clunks on the double fence. See us fly low over the motorway.

"Angels up," says Grandad.

ACKNOWLEDGEMENTS

Thanks to Marion Lloyd and Dan Amos for guiding me through these chilly Quarry waters.